Denton

Hathaway House, Book 4

Dale Mayer

Books in This Series:

Aaron, Book 1
Brock, Book 2
Cole, Book 3
Denton, Book 4
Elliot, Book 5
Finn, Book 6

DENTON: HATHAWAY HOUSE, BOOK 4
Dale Mayer
Valley Publishing Ltd.

Copyright © 2019

This is a work of fiction. Names, characters, places, brands, media, and incidents are either the product of the author's imagination or are used fictitiously. Any resemblance to actual events, locales, or persons, living or dead, is entirely coincidental.

ISBN-13: 978-1-773361-57-4
Print Edition

About This Book

Welcome to Hathaway House, a heartwarming military romance series from USA TODAY best-selling author Dale Mayer. Here you'll meet a whole new group of friends, along with a few favorite characters from Heroes for Hire. Instead of action, you'll find emotion. Instead of suspense, you'll find healing. Instead of romance, ... oh, wait. ... There is romance—of course!

Welcome to Hathaway House. Rehab Center. Safe Haven. Second chance at life and love.

Navy SEAL Denton Hamilton has checked himself into Hathaway House, hoping for a fraction of the results his friends have gotten at the rehab center. Now missing a rib, muscles and a portion of his stomach, as well as suffering from PTSD, Denton would be happy to have his physical self healed. He's not so sure he'll ever get his mental health back, and finding a woman who'll have him now—as his friends have been lucky enough to do—is out of the question. Who would be willing to love a man like him?

Administrative Assistant Hannah Forsythe helps Dani run Hathaway House. A loner at heart, she's drawn to Denton's struggle and dismayed at his belief that no one could ever love him. But when an ill-advised observation she makes has unexpected consequences for Denton's recovery, Hannah's only choice is to separate herself from him to help him progress without her.

As time passes, Hannah wonders if her choice has cost

her everything she's ever wanted or whether Denton can work through his feelings to give them both their happy ending at Hathaway House.

Sign up to be notified of all Dale's releases here!

https://smarturl.it/DaleNews

Prologue

D ENTON HAMILTON STARED at his email in disbelief. He'd heard so much about Hathaway House from Brock and Cole that Denton had been living in a fantasy world, hoping a miracle would happen and he'd have a chance to join his friends at the same center.

But the costs ... they were horrific.

He'd applied anyway. Made his case, knowing they took on a certain number of pro bono cases, and had hoped and waited.

He pulled out his cell phone and called Brock. It rang several times, then went to voice mail. He tried Cole.

"Denton, what's up?"

The curiosity in his friend's voice was justified. They'd been on the phone only a few minutes earlier. "I got in," Denton croaked, his voice clogging up. He cleared his throat several times, then repeated, "I got into Hathaway House. They have a bed for me." His voice rose at the end as the words in front of him finally settled in. "I'm coming there, Cole. I'll be there next week. We'll be together again."

"Holy crap, are you serious? That's the best news I've heard in a long time," Cole said warmly. "Wait until you see this place. You'll love it." He paused, then added in a teasing voice, "And you'll love the women."

"Nah, I'm not coming there for that. Besides, just because you and Brock found the perfect ladies for your lives, that doesn't mean Cupid is smiling in my direction. No, I'm happy to know I'm coming to Hathaway House and getting my best chance at regaining my strength and my health."

"Maybe so, but in this place, miracles do happen. I got mine. I know there is one here just for you."

Chapter 1

D ENTON HAMILTON COULDN'T believe his luck. His life had a tendency to go off the rails on a regular basis, so when good things happened, he always tried to stop and make a point of recognizing the moment. In this case, arriving at Hathaway House was beyond good luck. He hadn't had the funds to pay his own way, so when the benefactor money had been offered, he'd been over the moon. Both Brock and Cole were already there, and that made the trip all that much sweeter.

His brothers in arms were no longer big strapping men, ready to take on the world, like when they had first met. Now both of them were broken and damaged, nowhere near the men they were when they had first signed up for the military to train as SEALs. Still, Denton knew they had improved at Hathaway, and he was fully prepared to do what he could to improve his own physical health.

He was missing a ton of muscles, and his right calf was a mess. He would likely never do any heavy lifting again because he'd lost some back muscles to rebuild those calf muscles, plus, he was missing a bottom rib and part of his stomach. Food sensitivities were now a thing of everyday life as were blood sugar issues ... Life could be a whole lot worse. The right calf muscles ... those were traumatizing.

Waking up the first time with his right leg a mess had

been a hell of a shock. Who knew so many muscles were required to get that leg moving properly, not to mention doing simple things like climbing stairs? On top of that, he had also lost the baby toe on his left foot. He felt like a real idiot anytime he complained about it. The doctor had just chuckled and told him that missing toes meant relearning to walk again. But he had lost just one, and it shouldn't cause him that much trouble.

So, for now, a cane was his best friend. In the meantime, his goal was to return to be as fit as he could. He had to build up his right leg, and he had to build up his back. But he still counted himself lucky. He would do his best to make sure that whoever paid for him to come to Hathaway House wouldn't regret choosing him.

"Thank you so much for the ride," he said to the man beside him.

Dr. Wiseman smiled. "You're welcome. I'm always happy to deliver somebody here. It doesn't happen often enough. You're blessed that you are here."

"And I know it." He shook his head. "I'm not even sure how I made the cut. I don't have any money. Apparently, the center has donors, and one of them paid for my transfer and medical costs. The military said I'd been through everything they could do, but my leg is still useless. I hope all this is worth it."

"Not useless." The doctor shook his head. "It needs a lot of work, and the latest round of surgeries will take a lot of effort on your part to rebuild that leg. But the necessary muscles have been reattached. They need time to heal." Wiseman parked the car, exited, came around to Denton's side and opened the door. "This is only my second visit here," he said. "I'm looking forward to seeing the place again."

"I do appreciate the ride. I wasn't sure how all this would work."

"Sometimes the world works in mysterious ways," Dr. Wiseman said. He gave Denton a big smile. "Don't knock it. You're here. Make the most of it."

"I promise I'll do that much."

If Denton's reply was a little too emphatic, it was to be expected. He felt a little overwhelmed, truth be told. All those months and months of surgeries and the recoveries thereafter, seemed like a never-ending road where standing on his own two feet would be not only impossible, but also something that only the truly rich could afford. Not even the military had that much when it came to ongoing medical assistance. If Denton had stayed at the VA Hospital, he could have had all kinds of assistance, but none of it would have been as specialized as offered here at Hathaway House. Unlike some other people, he didn't have a problem being a charity case.

As Dr. Wiseman opened his car door, Denton struggled to his feet with the doctor's assistance. The front door to the medical center opened, and an orderly came toward them, pushing a wheelchair. Denton looked at it and sighed. "I'd hoped my wheelchair days were over."

Dr. Wiseman laughed. "You should be grateful that there is even a wheelchair for you. No overdoing it."

Once in the wheelchair, Denton turned to look up at Dr. Wiseman. "I don't have a problem accepting help. I was raised by a single mom. I learned from her. When she needed something done or when she needed something for me, she didn't care. She would ask people for help, or she would barter for what she needed. She was an expert at that.

Pride was never an issue for her." He shook his head. "Pride will never be an issue for me. I'm just too damn grateful to be alive."

"Good." Dr. Wiseman squeezed Denton's shoulder and walked beside him as the orderly pushed the wheelchair along the ramp. "There's a lot of people here. They come from all walks of life, all suffering traumatic events. Make sure you talk about your nightmares."

He nodded. "Will they ever go away?"

"PTSD is something a lot of men and women deal with. Military veterans are all over the world. Anybody who's been through the sort of traumatic experiences you have, well, it's to be expected. Let's just say, it's not necessarily forever. Having the right attitude and finding a strong positive support system are ways to improve your life and to help ease the traumatic stress of what you've been through."

At the front doors, he pushed a button, and both glass-paneled doors opened wide to allow the wheelchair through.

"Ah. There she is—Dani Hathaway."

Dani came around the front counter and shook the doctor's hand. "I'm so glad you came back for a visit."

"Thought I'd visit a couple of my favorite patients while I'm here."

Dani turned her gaze to Denton, and he shook her hand.

"Welcome to Hathaway House, Denton," she said brightly.

He answered simply and honestly. "Thanks. I'm glad to be here."

She smiled. "I believe two men are here who can't wait to see you."

Denton brightened. "I was so afraid they'd be gone before I got here, and I wouldn't get to see them," he confessed.

"Nope. They're waiting for you. However, we do have to get you through a quick orientation before you have time for yourself and them. So let's get you to your room."

She spoke to the orderly pushing his wheelchair. "George, would you take Denton to Room 73, please?" She looked back at Denton. "I'll be there shortly."

As he was wheeled away, he called over his shoulder, "Thanks again for the ride, Dr. Wiseman."

"No problem," he replied. "Good luck!"

As they rolled through wide, spacious hallways, Denton twisted around to look up at George. "How long have you worked here?"

"Forever," the orderly replied wryly. "It seems like forever."

Denton winced. That wasn't what he'd hoped to hear. "It's that bad?"

George's laughter rolled free. "No, not at all. I've been here since the place first opened. I came on board when Dani's father was still figuring out how to make this place into a working, viable business. That was ten years ago, at least, and I'm still here. I don't plan on leaving anytime soon."

Ten years. Denton sighed in relief. "That's good to know. I thought for a minute there you were saying this wasn't a good place to be."

He chuckled. "Just the opposite. You'll see a lot of people who have been here a long time." He turned a corner. "You're down on this side. I believe your buddies are on the other side though."

"Is that a big issue? Surely we can go back and forth to

see each other?"

"Absolutely not a problem. They're more mobile than you are."

"And I'll be catching up real fast—at least as fast as I can," he vowed, eager to get started.

"Not too fast though," George cautioned. "That's the worst thing you could do. Talk to Cole about that. You'll end up with a setback that'll take you even longer to recover from."

Denton's excitement disappeared. "So how do I do this? I want to make the most of my stay. I don't want to go too fast and have a setback, and I don't want to go too slow so that whoever pitched in to bring me here feels like they made the wrong choice."

"Don't you worry about that," George said. "Everybody here has an equal chance. There's no report card. There is no better or best. You must listen to your doctors and your body. And everybody's system, injuries, and mental state are all different. It's really important that you be true to yourself."

On that note, George pushed Denton through an open door. "This is your private room, with your own bathroom and a full shower. And your view overlooks the horse pastures."

"Cole said something about horses, and we can spend time with them," Denton said, enthralled. "And Brock talks about being with the animals in the vet clinic all the time." Denton shook his head. "Is that true?"

George nodded. "Stan runs the veterinary clinic on the lower level. We have a lot of animals in similar situations as our human patients. Some are in need of prosthetic limbs and special surgeries, and they are religiously cared for. Stan and Dani also do special rescues, and we keep the animals until we get them adopted out. You'll find several dogs visiting upstairs. They're comfort animals, so they will come around to make you feel not quite so alone. When you're capable physically, you can go downstairs to see Stan and meet the other animals. He's always got an animal that needs a hug. Because, like you, they've suffered enough."

Denton nodded, feeling a bit emotional.

George motioned to the bed. "Do you need any help getting on the bed?"

He spoke in such a commonplace tone of voice, Denton didn't take offense. "I think I should get there just fine. I have been doing decently enough, but my progress has slowed."

"That's fairly typical. Everyone plateaus at one point or another." George walked to the closet and opened the door. "Extra blankets and towels are here, and you have a couple drawers and the clothes hangers to put away some personal items. The desk is right here if you need it for your laptop, and as you can see beside the bed, you have one of those tables you can swivel over and back as need be." He glanced around the room. "I think that's all you need to know about in here. If you don't have any other questions, I'll let you settle in. Hannah should be here soon. She'll give you a tablet with further instructions and a timetable for your daily schedule."

Denton nodded. "I think I'm fine for the moment. Thank you so much."

He watched George leave. He hated to say he was a little nervous, but he was. Still, he was here. He made his way out of the wheelchair and sat down on the bed. He could walk but not far. Instead of walking around the bed, he rolled on his back and flipped his legs over, getting to the other side. Using the bed for support, he made the few steps to the window so he could look out. He smiled. A little filly was outside with a couple older horses in one great big pasture. Beautiful rolling hills. He shook his head and smiled widely. "This place is fantastic," he murmured.

Hearing a noise behind him, he turned a little too fast and had to grab hold of the window ledge.

"Easy there, tiger." Dani Hathaway stood in the doorway, her gaze concerned. Beside her was a tall, slim woman, holding a manila file folder and a tablet, wearing dark dress pants and a fitted white shirt.

"I'm fine." He smiled reassuringly. "You startled me."

Moving carefully, he took a few steps to the bed and sat down. With a lot of effort, he shifted back to lean against the headboard.

Dani smiled. "This is Hannah. She's here to get you settled in. I'll stop by a little later."

Hannah handed him a tablet and a notebook. "The notebook is for you, if you want to jot down any goals, any progress you want to keep track of, notes for yourself, whatever you like," she said. "Here is a pen and more are always at the front desk. The tablet gives you information on your team and your daily schedule. We have quite a system here. You don't have one practitioner. You will have five."

Denton's eyebrows rose at that thought. Then he looked at the screen and saw not only a short biography but a photograph along with the list of experiences and specialties of each medical professional. Dani was thorough, if nothing else.

Hannah continued. "If you check the Schedule tab at the top, you will see your daily events. It is not the same for everybody. The same team works on multiple patients a day and sometimes twice as many as that in a week. Everybody shuffles now and again, when we make changes. Also, you won't have the same physiotherapist. You will have several."

He glanced at her. "Is there a reason for that?"

She nodded. "That way, fresh eyes can see from different perspectives what a patient needs."

He nodded. "That makes sense."

She smiled at him, then handed him a cell phone. "This is yours. It has all your team members' numbers programmed in. Anytime you need any of us, including myself," she said, "you can call. It doesn't matter what time of day or night. Your team, in particular, happens to all live on-site."

He nodded and scrolled through the list. "Brock's on my team though, right?"

She laughed. "No, Brock's not on your team. Only employees are on your team. I understand that you, Brock and Cole are great friends." Something strange flickered through her voice as she said that.

He glanced at her, wondering what that was about. "We are. The three of us were inseparable."

"Good. Feel free to call them any time. If you look, you'll see both their numbers programmed in your phone on a secondary contact list. Okay, I'll explain the meals and how that works for you, but I'm sure they'll fill you in with a lot more as soon as they get a chance to see you."

So much information tumbled out of Hannah's mouth, Denton struggled to keep up. His expression must have given him away because she laughed when she came to a stopping point.

"I know I've dumped a lot on you, but it's not that bad. Everything I said is also written in here." She handed him a folder.

"Oh, thank God," he said. "I was so afraid I wouldn't remember."

"Not at all."

They shared grins.

She turned and walked toward the door. "I suggest you take a little time to get accustomed to your surroundings," she said. "In that folder is a map of the ground floor. Downstairs is a vet clinic. The public comes and goes on a regular basis to see the vet, to visit the animal patients. Some of the animals are permanent residents, and some are here for only short-term help. But all of them need as much loving care as any of the people in this place can give."

"Just like the patients." He liked the sound of that. "And I can go down there?"

"Eventually. Brock or Cole can take you in a day or two." At the doorway she stopped and faced him. "I do want to caution you. Please don't rush anything. Take your time. The move alone to transfer you here is hard on your body. You need time to adjust, so please honor that and give your body the time it needs."

He nodded soberly. "I can do that. I wouldn't want anything to set back my progress."

She gave him the sweetest smile. "I know you'll do your best."

And damn if there wasn't something special about her that made him want to do just that.

Chapter 2

HANNAH STEPPED INTO the hallway. Denton appeared to be a little overwhelmed with all the information she'd given him. She decided to come back later to see how he was doing. It was a lot to take in. This kind of medical center was a new experience for everyone, including the staff. Adjustment took a while. Patients needed time to settle in, as soon as possible, and to get into a routine.

She walked to the front desk and poked her head into Dani's office. "I'm done with Denton but will check again later today. The poor guy looked a little lost. Maybe if you get a chance, stop by this afternoon."

Dani looked up and smiled. "I can do that. You have definitely been helpful, taking over some of this work for me."

"Anything I can do to help. You're overworked. You should have a full-time assistant for yourself." Hannah smiled and withdrew.

Dani worked harder than anybody she'd ever seen before. Of course, it was her place, so it made sense. And she probably worked the hardest at keeping the staff and the patients happy. Obviously, there would always be personality conflicts and the occasional butting of heads, but in general, this place worked relatively smoothly.

Hannah had had experience in other medical offices,

including a doctor's office and a medical clinic in Houston. She certainly preferred working here. She'd only been at Hathaway House one year, and it had taken a few weeks to get into the Hathaway House mind-set and a few more weeks to realize how freeing it was to be here. The fact that the animals were here as well helped tremendously.

Thinking of the animals reminded her of something. She quickly jotted a note to herself. The next time she went shopping, she'd get a couple dog beds. That way she could have a few more of the animals upstairs on a regular basis. The patients appreciated having them around, and it wasn't always easy for patients to go downstairs. One of her jobs was to bring various animals from the clinic to visit the patients upstairs. She tended to use her various scheduled breaks throughout the day to find people who needed a one-on-one animal visit. This was especially true for the animals. Seeing too many people all at once was often stressful for them.

Hannah had three animals that she looked after on a regular basis and tracked when they were picked up by patients and taken away. If she'd had the chance, she'd have kept them all for herself. But understanding the animals were doing a very important job here made it easier to share them.

Some animals—like Chickie, the tiny partially crippled dog that appeared to get around in everyone's arms rather than walking—were a good example of that. He had water and food and a bed at the front counter and in the back area of the ground floor. But he was often cuddled up with somebody who needed it. And it was probably better that way as Chickie was very small and didn't move very well. The worst thing would be to have animals running loose, tripping up people on crutches or getting in the way of wheelchairs. Hathaway House employees didn't want any of the humans or the animals to get injured on-site either.

But something was very special about Chickie. He also had a supersensitive stomach, and although they warned everybody not to feed him, somehow his tummy was always a little upset. She wasn't sure if he was nibbling on crumbs off the floor or if somebody was secretly feeding him.

Helga was another example. She was a beautiful young Newfoundland, missing a leg. Her prosthetic limb was constantly undergoing design upgrades, everybody coming up with suggestions to make it work better for her. Helga herself didn't seem to care. The joint moved and rolled as she needed it to, and other than that, she was happy.

This group had been amazingly helpful in getting animals back on their feet. Chickie didn't have prosthetic limbs because his legs were quite crippled, and he had nowhere near the mobility that a lot of the other animals did. Being small made it easier as he required a lot more assistance.

Helga was huge, and as such she was appreciated by the men who were a little too afraid of hurting Chickie. The ones who loved Chickie simply carried him around like a baby.

Chickie belonged to the center, and Stan kept up regular medical treatments to keep him healthy. Hannah didn't understand how Dani had the time or the influx of funds to funnel monies in so many different directions, but she managed to get enough to cover what was needed. Hannah knew finding donors was a constant challenge, but Dani did it. She had a lot of benefactors who she could call in to get assistance for people who needed specialized medical help but couldn't afford to come here. And when one healed and moved on, then she opened the waiting list and brought in the next person needing their special rehabilitation efforts. It was a good system.

Dani also kept horses on the property. Most were refugee rescue horses. Some were damaged, but some were older and had no place in the regular world anymore. Dani was a horse lover, and Hannah didn't think Dani would ever turn away a horse. They had six right now. But unlike the dogs with a life expectancy of about twelve to fifteen years, horses often lived to their mid-twenties. The commitment was a lot longer.

Hannah had the title of administrative assistant, but really she was a jack-of-all-trades. She was a cross between Dani's assistant and the substitute front receptionist, plus she did some bookkeeping. And truth be told, she was good with that. There was certainly nothing boring about this job.

Her phone was ringing as she walked behind the front counter.

"Hey, Hannah. Do you have a moment?"

"Sure Stan, I'll be right down."

She hung up the phone and checked to see where Chickie was. He was curled up in his bed, looking darn tired. She decided to leave him where he was. He had done the rounds this morning with her, and he was certainly entitled to a nap. She grabbed a coffee cup, filled it and headed downstairs to see Stan.

The vet clinic was a mess. Several dogs in the reception area were struggling with their owners. In the center of the chaos was a cat, glaring at everybody.

Hannah stared at the cat. "So who's this guy?"

"We're not exactly sure."

Hannah looked at the vet's receptionist. "What? Didn't he have an appointment?"

Rebecca stood behind her desk. "No, and I didn't see who he came in with either. I have no idea. He doesn't look to be injured in any way."

Stepping between the dogs and cat, Stan crouched down. The cat took one look and jumped onto Stan's shoulders. Stan laughed. "Well, he's a friendly fellow."

"Very." Hannah studied the cat for a moment. "He's not scared of the dogs, and he seems to like the noise."

Stan glanced over at her with a knowing look. "You've been trying to get a therapy cat upstairs since forever."

She shrugged sheepishly. "It seems hardly fair that we have therapy dogs, but no cats."

He nodded. "We'll have to give this wonderful cat a checkup before we can let him around the human patients. But I was thinking of you and upstairs."

She stroked the feline, who seemed to like all the humans so far. "He's a beauty. He's almost bobcat size, isn't he?"

Stan nodded. "I wouldn't be surprised if something wild was in his heritage. He is really big."

She gently scratched behind his ears, and the huge cat's rumble filled the room.

"Good Lord," Stan said. "That's quite the engine."

She smiled. "You have to check him out real fast, Stan. I could use him upstairs." She turned to look at all the dogs sniffing the cat. She smiled. "Looks like you have a full day as it is."

Stan nodded, lifted the cat off his shoulders and handed him to Hannah as his temporary assistant. "Isn't that the truth?"

Hannah stepped out of Stan's way as he led one of the dogs with its owner into a treatment room. The cat gracefully jumped from Hannah's arms and onto the reception desk. Hannah smiled at the big cat, busy inspecting Rebecca's workspace.

"Is it usual to have them this calm at the clinic?"

Rebecca shook her head. "No. Usually they come in hissing at everything in sight."

"Well, this guy is certainly not doing that."

Rebecca stood and picked up the cat. "I'll take him to the back. That'll help the dogs calm down."

Hannah nodded and watched as the huge cat stared at her, his eyes glowing until he was out of the room.

She turned to the other people sitting in the waiting room. "Did any of you see the cat arrive?"

Two people shook their heads.

"No, suddenly he was just here. With all the chaos with the dogs, I didn't notice where the cat came from," the older woman replied.

Hannah looked down the long hallway. "It's possible he came in from the barn area." She headed that way to look, but the stalls were all empty, and the doors were closed. Mystified, she headed upstairs. She popped into Dani's doorway and explained the scenario.

Dani laughed. "So the center is so good that animals are coming in on their own now, are they?"

The two women laughed, and then Hannah returned to her office. They never knew what the next unusual scenario would be at this crazy job. And she wouldn't change it for anything.

Her cell phone rang within minutes of her sitting down. She groaned. "Good thing my workload is easier today."

She glanced down to see the caller was Denton. "Denton Hamilton, what can I do for you?"

His hesitant voice came through. "I hate to be a bother, but I've tried calling Brock and Cole, but neither call appears to be going through."

She frowned. "That's odd. I'll bring the numbers down myself, and we can double-check them." She grabbed her checklist and headed toward Denton's room.

He sat on his bed, his legs hanging over the edge. He had switched to shorts, perhaps for some of the medical tests or physical therapy or just to feel more comfortable. But to see his calf mangled like that, she fought back a wave of sympathy. His foot was also completely covered in scar tissue, and it appeared to be missing part of a joint. She glanced at his face and realized he had watched her reaction.

He kicked out his bum leg. "What do you think?"

She shrugged and sent him a gentle smile. "I've seen worse."

He looked at her, his gaze searching her face until he realized she was serious, and he relaxed. "I guess I don't have to hide it, do I?"

She shook her head. "Never. Please do not hide anything. Find a level of comfort, and learn to live with it. You can relax. We've all seen much worse injuries. We'll do the best we can to help you get back to a normal life."

He smiled. "And part of that is contacting my friends." He held out his phone.

She checked to see if she'd switched some of the digits. "I'm so sorry. I'm mildly dyslexic, and phone numbers are sometimes a challenge." She carefully brought up each of the numbers, then checked her list, and together they watched as she put in the right numbers.

"Try that now." Inside, she winced at her mistake. She hadn't done that for a while. But when she got tired or busy, her brain automatically switched numbers on her. It was frustrating.

Denton tried Brock first, and when the man answered, she watched happiness bloom across Denton's face. He waved at her and mouthed the words, *Thank you.*

She nodded, gave him a smile and turned to leave. Behind her, she could hear him chatting with Brock. There was such love and friendship in his voice, and she was happy for them. It also reminded her how lacking her own life was in those two areas. Love, well, she hadn't found it yet. However, she'd made more friends since arriving at the center than she had ever had in her life. But she didn't have any friends from school or from college. She didn't have any long-term friendships beyond this last year. She'd tried hard enough to make some, but it never seemed to work out. She never had the knack for it. Apparently, of all the things wrong with Denton, his ability to make and keep friends was not one of them.

"HEY, BUDDY ... Guess who's finally landed?" Denton asked when Brock answered.

Brock laughed and cheered. "What room are you in? I'll come to you."

Denton gave Brock the room number and ended the call. Denton thought about the look he'd seen on Hannah's face when she exited the room. Something in her voice, something in her expression, he didn't quite recognize.

Something akin to hesitation, as if she wanted to stay longer. He wished he could call her back. He didn't know what, if anything, was wrong. But he'd spent a lot of time alone himself, wishing that somebody would talk to him. Sometimes he had to admit the last few months at the hospital had been hard. He'd been inundated with people. But not one of them had been a friend. Not one of them had been a Brock or a Cole. His friends had been here, dealing with their own rehab, and Denton had been there, dealing with his. However, now he'd passed through one stage and had made it to the next. Although he was following in their footsteps, he knew that these guys would always give him a helping hand. That was what friends did. And he never doubted them.

Together they'd seen some pretty ugly things. They'd been on some dangerous missions. They'd done some incredibly grueling training and had pushed themselves to the limit, and still they'd survived. Not just that but they'd excelled. He wasn't ashamed or worried about anything he'd done in his past. That his future was unknown, and therefore a little unnerving, was true. But he hoped he didn't have to face that alone either. And again, Brock and Cole were there ahead of Denton to show him the way.

He could hear footsteps coming down the hallway. He wasn't sure if someone was headed toward him or not, but he got excited nonetheless.

Suddenly a familiar head popped around the corner of his doorway, and with a big grin on his face, Brock stepped into the room. "I am glad to see you're here finally!"

Denton shook his head. "I tried to get here earlier, honest. But recovering from my surgeries was a never-ending process, and I couldn't seem to get clear of it."

Brock nodded in understanding. "We've been there, done that." He motioned at the bare leg Denton had hanging off the edge of the bed. "Looks pretty gnarly, man."

Denton laughed at his slang. "It is gnarly. But hopefully here we can build it up. Who knew they could take muscles off your back and reattach them somewhere else?"

"Modern medicine is a beautiful thing, man." Brock's back and side were severely damaged. "My injuries weren't much better. Half my body is scar tissue, with half a cheek missing." But he said it with a big grin and a shrug, as if to say, *What the hell? It's what the cards are, and we must live with them.*

Brock had always been like that, until his accident. Denton nodded. "It's not exactly where I thought we'd end up though."

"We should have. The lives we led, the situations we were in, if we'd had even a basic understanding of how many of our fellow soldiers ended up like this, it wouldn't seem so odd."

"Maybe we chose not to look too closely?"

"Absolutely." Brock glanced around the room. "This place is great. You'll love it here. If you work hard, you will excel, and in no time, you'll see a huge difference."

"I'm counting on it," Denton said in a quiet voice. "A lot of extra funding had to be put into place to get me here. I'm looking to make the most of the opportunity."

Brock stared at him for a long moment, before giving a sharp nod. "You've always been the one who showed gratitude and understanding about how lucky you were. While I was griping about circumstances, you'd put that sunny smile on your face and say, *We are good.*" He shook his head. "Honestly, that'll hold you in good stead here."

Denton laughed. "Look what I got." He held up the map in his hand. "Hannah gave this to me."

"Hannah? Not Dani?"

Denton shook his head.

"Hannah's been here for a while, but she's stepping up to take some of Dani's extra workload apparently."

"Both of them made sure I was settled into my room."

"Well, lucky you. Hannah's a sweetie."

"And Dani isn't?"

"Oh, she is too, but she's taken. Hannah's single."

Denton rocked back slightly and looked up at Brock. "What? Is there a matchmaking service here too?"

"No, but once you're past that intensive medical level, and you're back on your feet, it's automatic for your mind to return to other activities besides getting from point A to point B without the help of crutches and a wheelchair."

Denton smirked. "And you are always one to lead the pack in that direction." He studied Brock for a long moment, assessing the impish grin but also the warm light in his gaze. "So spill then. Who is she?"

Brock looked at him sheepishly. "Her name is Sidney. She's one of the massage therapists here."

"Is it serious?"

Brock nodded. "Serious as I can make it. I've got another month here, then I'm graduating forward."

Inside, Denton took that as a visceral hit. He winced. "I was kind of hoping for more than a month, if not six months."

"I won't be far way," Brock said. "I'll be staying in Dallas. Sidney will continue working here, and I'm looking for a job in town. We'll see what we can do about living arrangements."

"Wow, that is serious."

Brock nodded. "When you find the right woman"—he took a deep breath—"and you come so close to losing your life, you don't mess around. I love her. Like, I *really* love her." He opened his arms and grinned sheepishly. "And after I was injured, I never thought I'd see such a day come. But she doesn't mind the scars. She doesn't care about the broken body. She's truly special."

"Then you are very lucky," Denton said. "I think we all go through that stage, thinking we're done with relationships, especially when we wake up in bed, broken, screaming in the middle the night with flashbacks causing our bodies to swim in sweat and the fear raging up our throats."

"My nightmares were never as bad as yours. I get a few, but they don't torment me quite so bad. Make sure you talk to the therapist about that. Post-traumatic stress syndrome is nothing to fool around with."

"I know. I've been keeping it under control, but sometimes ..."

"Sometimes life gets to be too much." He nodded in understanding. "Like I said, make sure you talk to the therapist about it. Everybody here does such a marvelous job in their own field. It's amazing how much progress we're all making."

"What about Cole? Where is he? Is he still playing catch-up?"

"Hell no," Brock said. "He's doing much better now too. He had a rough beginning, but he's come a long way."

"*Lovely*. I'm so far behind both of you that there is no point in playing catch-up."

Brock stepped into the hallway, returning a moment later with a wheelchair. "That's not important. What matters is understanding your limits and sticking to them. I was always leapfrogging ahead, doing too much, too fast. Cole was always playing catch-up, scared that what he did wasn't enough. Yet, you need to be content to do what you can do so you can be happy with yourself for the rest of your life."

He smiled. "While you're here, follow that same pattern. You will progress at a pace that's right for you. Don't worry about anyone else. Progress of any kind might look like a complete impossibility—particularly when you see so many people months ahead of you into their rehab. But when you look back on your own progress, you'll be amazed." He patted the wheelchair. "One of the things you don't want is to overdo it. That lesson I learned from Cole, who ended up back in the hospital only a few days after he got here. Hop on, and let's go for a ride."

Slowly, but under his own strength, Denton made his way to sit in the wheelchair, his legs on the footrests, and with a sense of finally coming home that he hadn't had in so long, he let his best buddy take him from his room for a tour of the place.

As they turned a corner, Hannah came toward them down the hallway. She grinned. "Now that looks like a perfect idea for this morning. Make sure you don't take him too far or make him do too much," she cautioned Brock.

He gave her a smile. "I would never do anything to hurt this guy."

Denton twisted to look behind them as she continued on.

Brock leaned down and whispered in his ear, "See? Like I said … Hannah's hot. She's smart, and you're definitely interested."

Denton sank back into the wheelchair. "I might be interested, but I don't plan to do anything about it. I'm here to heal, and that's where I'll put my focus."

Brock whistled a light, happy tune but then paused for a

moment. "You can do what you want, but when life smacks you upside the head, you can't ignore it. All you can do is let fate play a hand and see where you land."

Chapter 3

AT THE END of the hallway, Hannah stopped and looked over her shoulder to see the two men chuckling together. She smiled and murmured, "If nothing else, just having friends around would help."

"Talking to yourself, Hannah?" Shane's voice came from behind her. "That's not a good sign at your age." He shook his head. "Of course, if you're talking about the two strapping men who went down that hallway, then maybe your comment was about something important."

She flushed and shook her head. "I was saying how having friends around would help Denton heal faster. To have them as role models and to have their support."

"We all need friends."

She nodded. "I can't say I've had a ton in my lifetime. And to see what these men have together is a unique experience for me."

"I think their circumstances, coupled with what they've been through, have helped build a bond most of us can't access."

"And yet his buddies, Cole and Brock, found partners here at the center," she said slowly. "And so, either they opened that existing relationship to let others in or they had the capacity to have more than just one or two friends."

He stopped and studied her for a long moment. "You've

made friends since you've been here, right?"

She laughed. "Yes, absolutely." Of course, they weren't close friends. "I don't have friends from grade school. I barely remember anybody I went to college with. Some people have friends who span twenty to thirty years. How did they do that? How do you find people you're willing to stay in contact with all those years? That's such a gift. I think these three have it. And maybe, I realize I wish I had something like that."

He seemed to follow her rambling thoughts without any trouble. He smiled and nodded. "I've seen that happen myself. My parents have friends spanning fifty years. But I never had any long-term friends either. I made friends in college, and I've stayed in contact with a few of those but more for networking, in case I ever need another job. That way, I always know who to contact and can say, 'Hey, what's happening in your corner of the world?'" He grinned at her. "My real friends are here. I've been here for close to six years straight now, and I've certainly made more friends in those years than from before. You've only been here a year. I've seen you make friends, but they don't necessarily meet the criteria of long-term friendship."

"I hear you. It would be nice to see where I am in five or seven years. I'd like to have a friend so I can look back when I'm old and gray and smile because I've known somebody else for all that time. And they know me as well as I know them."

"I think a lot of times those become partners. It's not that we can't have male friends or female friends, but often a friend like that is the person who we fall in love with. The person who we plan to stay with, the person who we want to be with for the rest of our lives. To become a best friend.

And that's who you get to spend your time with and smile at and hold hands with when you're in your rocking chairs, many years down the road."

She grinned. "That's a nice picture. I know a lot of people would cringe at the thought, but imagining sitting on a rocking chair fifty years in the future and holding my husband's hand makes me smile and sigh. To think that somebody could know me and love me and want to be with me for that length of time—well, that's just special."

"I think Dani's found that with Aaron," Shane said. "I think Brock and Sidney have found that." He smiled. "I'm not too sure yet, but Sandra may have found the exact same thing in Cole too." He glanced up and down the hallway. "It's something I've never seen here before, but definitely a love bug is going on. Maybe Cupid moved in." He shrugged. "I don't know what it is, but there's been a change. Maybe you need to stay open to the idea, and you'll find somebody to love yourself."

He wrapped an arm around her shoulders and gave her a gentle hug. And then he walked away, leaving her alone with that thought.

She realized one thing—Shane was one good friend she'd made while here.

IT WAS HARD to find anything more perfect than this morning. Finally seeing Brock. Finally being at the center, a place Denton had tried so hard to get into for so long. Denton's heart was overwhelmed with joy and satisfaction. He'd achieved this. No, not all on his own. But that didn't matter. He was here now. Brock was here now and hopefully would be for another couple months. But like he had said, he would stay close. And that was like having family all over again.

Denton gave a happy sigh and settled back for the tour. Brock took him through the upstairs, which was the ground-floor level, showing him the nurses' station and all the physiotherapy rooms. Brock kept up his rambling conversation that was both easy and lighthearted. And it did a lot to help Denton relax. They bypassed Dani's office—whether on purpose or not, Denton didn't know—but Brock did wheel Denton past the front reception where Hannah was. The two men smiled at her.

"What's this?" She grinned and said teasingly, "Is the reception desk a tourist stop now?"

Brock nodded. "I figured I'd better show him all the places on limits and off-limits," he joked.

Denton raised an eyebrow. "I haven't heard about the off-limits places."

"That's because there aren't very many." Hannah shook her head. "How come you haven't taken him to pick up a cup of coffee for the tour?"

Denton looked up at his buddy. "What? You're gypping me out of a cup of coffee?"

With a chuckle, Brock turned the wheelchair in the opposite direction. "I was getting there—honest. I was getting there."

Denton watched as they came to a massive open dining-area space. A set of large retractable doors were open, creating one giant room with a massive deck outside, merged seamlessly together. Brock stopped right at the dining room entrance, so Denton could get a good look.

"This is the main hub of this place," Brock said. "Drinks

and snacks are always available. If you're on a special diet, then talk to your team about getting specific snacks available for you. There are three set mealtimes, but if you miss a meal and you're hungry, you can always talk to Dennis."

A large male behind the counter lifted his head and waved. He smiled and called out, "Hey, Brock ... did we get a new one?"

Brock laughed as he wheeled Denton closer. "Denton, this is Dennis. Anytime you need food, whether it's mealtime or not, he'll hook you up."

Dennis came around and shook Denton's hand. "Welcome."

Appreciating the camaraderie and openness of the place, Denton shook Dennis's hand. "Hannah said something about coffee?"

Dennis chuckled. "Where would we be without that brew?" He pointed to the side wall. "Brock can take you to our snack station. There's always coffee and tea, black and herbal. Hot chocolate too and juice. If you want something that we don't have, let me know, and I'll do my best to get it for you."

Brock wheeled them slowly through what was mostly an empty room. Some staff appeared to be having a meeting at a table at one end of the room, papers strewn across the tabletop, and a couple of patients sat at a table outside.

"The property looks unbelievable," Denton commented. "It's a unique setting."

"You don't know the half of it. Once you see the animals, you'll understand how special this place is."

They made it to the coffee bar where Brock poured two cups, set them on a tray and handed the tray to Denton to carry. "You hungry? There are cookies, cinnamon buns, or fruit."

Denton said, "I want a cinnamon bun," then laughed as Brock had already picked up two and added them to his tray.

"Now the only question you must answer is, sit inside or outside?"

"Is the tour over?"

"Nope. This is a midway stop."

Laughing and joking, the two moved outside to one of the largest tables on the deck. The sunshine and fresh air were spectacular. As Brock moved a dining chair so the wheelchair could pull right up to the table, Denton carefully lifted the tray to the table without any spills. He glanced up at Brock. "I was sure I would dump it."

"You wouldn't be the first to do that. It took me a long time to learn how to carry a tray while on crutches."

Denton shook his head. "I'm so not ready for that."

"I wasn't either," Brock said cheerfully.

Denton relaxed in his chair, enjoying an atmosphere that felt more like a vacation resort than an actual medical facility. "Staff and patients mingle all the time?"

"They can. They do have offices, and they have some separate meeting rooms, but they might as well come here, have fresh coffee and something to eat while having their meeting."

"And visitors?"

"They come too. All visitors must pass through the front doors, and they must sign in. You have to arrange for your visitors ahead of time to avoid interrupting your rehab schedule."

"That makes sense." Denton asked a few more questions but then fell silent as he took the first bite of his cinnamon bun. He shook his head and moaned. "Oh my God, this is so good."

Brock nodded. "Wait until you get to the meals. I will miss the food here."

Denton stared at him in astonishment. "Are you serious? Usually, in any kind of medical facility, the food is crappy."

"Not here." Brock ripped off a huge piece of cinnamon bun from the outside of his roll and ate it.

"There you are," a woman called out.

Brock glanced up, and the look in his eyes—a warm, almost melted look—had Denton studying Brock in surprise. A tall beautiful woman came around the table and reached out a hand. Brock grasped it.

Denton turned to the woman. "I gather you're Sidney."

Laughter rolled from her, and she nodded. "Nice to meet you. You must be the Denton I've heard so much about."

Denton winced. "All good things, I hope."

"Of course," she said with a smile. "I see Brock's giving you the tour."

Denton nodded. "I'm still hoping to meet up with Cole soon."

"You will," she said confidently. "He's doing his sessions right now. Maybe another half hour to forty-five minutes." She glanced at her watch. "Wow. Okay, it's almost lunchtime. The morning has disappeared faster than I expected." She glanced at Brock. "Are you two staying here for lunch, or are you giving him a tour down below after your coffee and then coming back?"

"We'll have our coffee and cinnamon buns, finish the tour and then we'll hopefully meet up with Cole for lunch here. I'll text him and make sure he'll be here." Brock looked up at her hopefully. "Can you join us too?"

"I have a meeting with the other therapists. If it runs late, then I won't make it. But if I finish on time, then I'll be happy to." She gave him a warm smile and then switched her gaze to Denton. "I trust you're here for all the right reasons. Be sure you make the most of your stay," she said cryptically, and then she pivoted and walked off.

Denton couldn't help but watch her as she left. She was beautiful and confident. His gaze flew back to Brock, who had a foolish smile on his lips. "You got it bad, don't you?"

"I got it bad. And for the first time in my life, I've found a partner whom I'm quite happy to spend the rest of my life with."

"Wow." Denton picked up his coffee mug and took a big drink. So many new and different things going on here. His mind had trouble grasping it all. His impression of Brock was still like the good old times before their trio had been injured. Though Denton had visited Brock when he was broken and then again just out of surgery, now he was a completely new man. "I'm really happy for you."

Brock grinned. "Hey, you probably haven't heard Cole's hooked up too."

Denton stared at him. "Cole?"

Brock nodded. "But that's Cole's tale to tell. So I'll let him fill you in." Brock bounced to his feet. "Drink up your coffee. We'll finish the tour and then come back for lunch."

Eager and still stunned by everything he'd seen and learned, Denton polished off his bun and washed it down with the last of his coffee. He looked at the tray. "Where do we put the dirty stuff?"

"You grab it, and I'll take you there." Once they'd dropped off their dishes, they headed into a wide hallway and stopped outside a large elevator door. Brock pushed the button.

"The animal clinic's downstairs, along with some other fun things."

Inside the elevator, Denton's mind spun. *Animals? Other things?* When the elevators opened, the hallway teemed with dogs.

Brock chortled. "Well, what's going on here?"

The receptionist glanced at them. "Hi, Brock. A property seizure was completely overrun with dogs in poor condition. We're waiting on another vet to come in, but the rescue people brought in all the animals at once. We're still sorting them out."

Sadness washed over Denton at the sight of the maltreated animals. Each one's fur was matted and dirty, and he could see scabs and sores. None appeared to have much spirit left within them. He glanced at the receptionist. "Are these all from the seizure?"

"We have twelve from the seizure, but over seventy animals were rescued."

He shook his head. "Is there anything we can do to help?"

The woman looked at him. "Have I seen you here before?"

"I'm Denton." He waved. "I just arrived."

She looked at him. "You probably shouldn't be doing very much then." She glanced at Brock for confirmation.

"He might not do very much yet, but he can certainly reach out a hand and help a scared animal," Brock said. He moved Denton into the center of the room. "Hang on. Let's see what Stan's up to and if he needs more volunteers."

Just then an older man in scrubs stepped from one of the rooms. His gaze landed on Denton and Brock and lit up.

"Hey, guys. Sorry, it's a bit chaotic right now." He turned to the receptionist. "Put these two into the cages. They've been checked over. Let's go through the rest of them one by one and get some treatments started."

Two other women came out of the back rooms. Denton watched as the assistants carefully moved several more dogs into the treatment rooms. He reached for a smaller one—some sort of shaggy-looking crossbreed that could barely see from the mop over its eyes—and smiled sadly when the dog cowered away. Denton immediately pulled back, then let the dog gather its courage just to sniff him on his own. The dog returned again after a few minutes, watched his fingers, and then a tiny tongue came out and licked them. He stroked the animal. "He's trembling in fear."

"Yes. It's been a long day for them already, and they've gone through a lot of trauma and shock. But now that they are here, they'll get fixed up and taken care of, and hopefully they'll all be fine."

As they watched, the vet techs came out again and led the bigger dogs into two different treatment rooms.

Brock reached for a German shepherd, lying on its side, and Denton could see bald patches and scars along its side. The shepherd lay there, staring at Brock with huge eyes. Brock scratched him gently behind the ears. "You'll be fine now, boy. You'll be just fine."

For Denton, it was one more shock to his system. He adored animals, all of them. And to see so many hurting, well ... he could feel a lump rising in his throat. "I want to help."

The receptionist stood from behind her desk, shuffling folders. She gave him a gentle smile. "And you certainly can. But one of the best things you can do is get strong enough so you can help yourself. And then you can take on as many volunteer hours in the vet clinic as you want to give."

He nodded. The woman had a valid point.

"The first batch is getting their checkups now," she said. "The rest of the day will be full of shampooing, a lot of fur clipping and many medical treatments. Now that the triage is essentially done, we know who needs treatment first."

Brock nodded. He and Brock stayed for another twenty minutes, gently petting and calming the animals still in the larger room. And while they waited, several other animals were switched out and collected. When they finally left to go upstairs, only four dogs were left that still needed to be checked over. "We'll come back later and see how they're all doing." He glanced down at Denton. "You ready to go?"

Swallowing hard, Denton gave a sharp nod. "Yes."

Quietly the two headed toward the elevator. As he was about to push the button, Brock stopped. "Oh, I got so caught up with the dogs, I forgot to show you what else is down here." He pushed the wheelchair farther down the hall and took a left. As he went, he pointed out the stalls, access to the barns, and the double doors that led out to the pastures. "But we want to go this way." And he took Denton in the other direction. There the double doors opened up to a huge patio and a massive pool.

Denton sat back and stared. A huge smile crept over his face. "Oh, wow. All I want to do is go in there, like, right now."

"And you will. As soon as you get the green light from your health team," Brock said. He pointed out the changing rooms and the hot tub.

Denton could see all the modifications on the pool to help people get in and out—even a motorized seat that moved up and down for those who needed it. "You don't see a pool like this in very many places."

"No. We certainly put it to good use though."

Denton scanned the water, watching three people splashing around. A man was doing laps, a woman sat on the pool's edge, and the other woman was treading water. Denton wasn't sure, but it looked like she didn't have any arms. He stared down at his bad leg and realized, yet again, how lucky he was. He wasn't helpless. And knew he could tread water in the pool without too much trouble. Then he remembered how some of his back muscles had been replaced in his right leg and wondered how that would affect his swimming.

"Don't worry about it."

It was as though Brock had read his mind.

"You'll do what you can do as fast as you can do it, and then you'll improve from that point on." Brock turned him around. "The stairs over there go up to the deck, where we were sitting for coffee before."

Denton nodded. "Too bad there isn't an elevator right here."

"You're right, there isn't, but we use the one back down the hall where we came downstairs. There is also a service elevator, but we're not allowed to use it unless there are exceptional circumstances."

"I guess there isn't that much need for another elevator. Because people don't use one for the vet clinic, correct?"

"Correct. The clinic has its own door on this lower level, and that's what the vet clients use."

Back at the elevator, Brock got them inside and upstairs. "I haven't heard from Cole, but I suggest, given the hour, that we pick a table."

"I'd like to see Cole over lunch, if we get the chance."

"You will, if Cole's in any physical shape to make it. If he's not, then we'll hit his room afterward."

At that thought, Denton fell silent. Because of course, what *he* wanted was only part of the equation. What Cole wanted and what Cole could do—well, that was a whole different story.

They made it back to the same table they'd used before, but now the room had filled up by half. Denton could smell delicious aromas as big bins of food were brought out for the buffet. "I can't believe I'm hungry."

"You need the food to rebuild. They do not cut corners here, and it's all good stuff."

"Denton? Is that you?" Cole raced toward Denton.

Tears stung his eyes. He opened his arms, and Cole threw his arms around him and gave him a huge hug. When he stepped back, Denton looked his buddy up and down.

"Oh, my God, I'm so glad to see you here," Cole said. "I was afraid you couldn't make it."

Denton was completely surprised to see Cole looking as well as he was. He wasn't as fit or as big or as strong and obviously not quite as healthy as Brock. But Cole was still miles away from where Denton currently was. He shook his head. Seeing his two buddies was like a look into his own future, where he might be in a month or two as compared to where he'd be in six months. "Damn. You look good, man."

Cole grinned at him. "It's you who looks good. We're so glad to have you here."

Chapter 4

HANNAH WONDERED WHAT it was about her new awareness that made her see the missing element in her life everywhere. She remembered, back in college, a pregnant woman saying that ever since she found out she was pregnant, all she saw was pregnant women around her. Maybe that was a good thing. Maybe it made her realize she wasn't alone in whatever condition she was in. Hannah seemed to understand how much her lack of friends had impacted her life now that all she saw were other groupings of friends.

Denton may have started this new process that she hadn't noticed earlier, after she'd seen him with Brock. And now Cole was with them. She sat at the far end of the deck, all alone like always. The other staff, although friendly, weren't necessarily friends. And when they did come together, it was usually over meetings or because they had patients to discuss and needed advice from one another. Still meetings but more informal.

After a year of being here, she hadn't made *close* friends. Sure, there were guys like Shane. Stan downstairs. She was friendly with Dani. But not to the point where Hannah arranged to have lunch with them every day. Maybe that was on her. Maybe she had messed up. Maybe she sent out some sort of vibe that said, *Stay back. I want to be alone.*

It's what she knew. And change was hard. Being alone was comfortable. At least it had been up until now. She didn't like it, but she wasn't sure that she *disliked* it enough to make the effort to change it.

Laughter came from the side of the deck where Denton and Brock and Cole sat, which brought her attention once again to the three men. They'd been friends since forever. Been through some of the most grueling training anybody had been through. When they saw one of their friends fall, the others had been there to help. But now that all three had fallen—physically injured, yet on the way to recovery—they were all here to help each other get through this chapter of their lives. It was incredible. It was amazing. It was uplifting.

It was also heartbreaking.

If she were in a car accident right now or some disease or illness overtook her system, who would help her get through the day?

She'd lose her job, and she wouldn't be able to pay her bills. Sure, she had decent medical insurance here, and she would get medical care, but she couldn't continue to live here. She'd have to find another place, and she'd be alone. She had no other friends in town or even close to town, and she would go through whatever healing process was required, either to recovery or to death … alone.

It was a terrifying thought.

As she'd never faced a major trauma, her lack of friends and family wasn't exactly something she'd had to face. But now that she looked at it closer, she didn't like the gap in her world. Unlike some people, who filled the emptiness in their lives with work and hobbies, she'd just closed the door and acknowledged that that part of her life didn't even exist. That wasn't good either. She stared at the coffee cup in her hand, studying the swirls of coffee at the bottom of the mug. Aimless. Confused. Insecure. Because throughout all this was the question: Why didn't she have friends? And that brought up the next question, which was: What was wrong with her?

She gave a heavy sigh, leaned back in her seat, raised her coffee cup and stared over it at the pasture. Many a day she'd sat here and smiled at the animals, enjoying the view, loving being part of this place. But right now it was hard to see the beauty. All she saw was a single horse in the pasture, which made her instinctively feel there should be two horses. Because, in her mind, she was certain the horse was lonely.

And if she felt the horse was lonely, clearly she was projecting her own loneliness onto the animal. And clearly she felt lonely because she was alone. The two didn't always go together. Often she enjoyed her own company, just have silence around her, that sense of comfort in her own space, but right now, she admitted she was lonely. But for how long had this been? As she kept the door closed on that whole compartment within herself, she wasn't exactly sure she had an answer. Now that she was wondering, however, it seemed like forever. She'd had various friends in school. But not friends she did anything with on the weekends or ones who discussed every detail of their lives with her.

She'd had a couple boyfriends but none lately. Most people preferred to be with a partner so they weren't alone. Her last relationship had only been so-so, and when it had broken off, she hadn't been upset. It was also why she hadn't been too worried about finding another relationship until she found somebody she really attracted to. No more settling.

So far, that hadn't happened. Until now. Until Denton. Hannah had to wonder if her interest was merely because of that vibrant energy, that sense of gratitude, that sense of *I can do this* which surrounded him and how he had attracted two such good friends. She saw no hint of ego or arrogance, which she was accustomed to seeing from so many people. Neither was there that brokenness inside that she'd seen a lot of. It was like he walked carefully through the middle of all that maze of emotions and did it very successfully. He had charisma. Was that why he had friends? Did he send out a welcoming energy to say, *You're a friend I haven't met yet?*

She wanted to know. At the same time, she was scared to become too friendly with him in case that spark of attraction wasn't mutual. What was it he had that allowed him to make and keep friends? And the people she worked with? What did they have that enabled them to have such good friendships?

Because they did. She saw the staff groupings but hadn't really *seen* them until now. She glanced at Denton once more to see the three men full of joy and laughter with such a sense of welcome and delight in being in each other's company. They'd all been through such hardships, and she was proud of them. Amazed at how well they had handled life when it had reached up and smacked them down.

Insight struck her like a lightning bolt. She wanted to be part of that circle.

As she watched them, Sidney joined them, placing a hand on Brock's shoulder. He looked up at her, and his smile didn't brighten, but it changed. It became more intimate, more loving. Sidney got inside that circle. Sidney had a bright, sunny personality, whereas Hannah was quietly reserved. She was happy to be around others but quite content to retire to her room all alone.

Sidney called out to somebody. Hannah watched as

Sandra walked over, for Cole. Sandra accepted his hand. He tugged her down and tucked her closer and whispered something in her ear. The other men chuckled, and Sandra blushed and rolled her eyes. Hannah was close enough to see the intimacy yet far enough to not hear the conversation. As she studied the five of them, she saw another aspect of Denton that she didn't understand.

He was clearly content to simply be there, content to watch his friends find partners. He didn't show any sign of being jealous or of feeling left out. Instead, his huge expanse of a smile said he was so grateful to be included.

Maybe that was it. Maybe she wasn't happy with her friend world as she wasn't included in much. She knew many people here, but she wasn't part of any inner circles. She was happy to be here—thankful even. But she wasn't particularly grateful for something special in her life. And that was sad.

In fact as she watched Denton for a while longer, she realized how empty her life truly was.

"YOU GUYS LOOK great together," Denton said warmly. "I never thought to see the two of you pair up with such beautiful women."

Brock smiled. "These women are beautiful on the inside as well as beautiful on the outside. I've thought about this. Maybe we had to get so empty inside so that there was room for them. I guess our lives were so full of people before, so many orders, so many routines, so many instructions, and so many things to do in a day that although we had time for relationships, there wasn't nearly as much room for them then as there is now."

"It's not just that," Cole added. "We weren't as welcoming of something at this level because of all the other stuff that filled our days. Our relationships were more superficial as well. That was all we had time for. But now look at us. It's a whole new world out there. And I, for one, want to make the most of it. I feel like I didn't lose ten years of my life but more like my life had gone by so fast I almost missed those ten years. I know the next ten will disappear almost as quickly. And I don't want them to go by in a blur, not knowing anything about what happened. I want to look back and know they were the foundation for the rest of my life. I want them to be happy years. I want to wake up in the morning and smile. I want to go to bed at night with peaceful dreams, not nightmares."

It was hard to miss the whisper of concern across Sandra's face. She squeezed Cole's shoulder gently.

He reached out and patted her hand. "I'm fine. Don't worry. The nightmares haven't started up again."

Denton could see the relief on her face.

"Just checking," she said quietly.

Denton nodded and smiled. "Sounds like nirvana, what you all have."

"That doesn't mean it's not available to you too, Denton," Sandra said. "Maybe you're not at the point yet where you can see the joy of what's to come."

He glanced down at his mangled leg and gave a shrug. "That's possible. It's hard to see anything yet." He raised his gaze and caught sight of Hannah sitting all alone on the other side of the deck. He had assumed she awaited somebody joining her. But now that her meal was done, she sat there alone, her mug in her hand, staring out over the pasture. It was the lonely look on her face that caught his attention. Surely she had friends here. He couldn't imagine working in a place like this without making lots of friends. Then again, he was an extrovert. He made friends easily, always had. He understood some people had to work at it. He always thought that was a shame. But the world was full of all kinds of people. He watched as she put the cup on the table, then pulled her knees to her chest and wrapped her arms around them. As if holding herself in and keeping the rest of the world out.

"Hey, Denton? You there, buddy?"

He pulled away his gaze and glanced at Brock. "I'm here. What did I miss?"

A knowing gaze crossed Brock's face, as he looked where Denton had been staring.

Denton shook his head. "Nothing there, Brock."

"There could be, if you want it to be," Brock said with a big grin.

Cole piped up. "I feel like I'm missing something now." His gaze slipped from one buddy to the other, as if looking for answers.

Denton smiled. "You're not missing anything, yet."

At that point the two women said goodbye to their partners and headed inside the dining hall and back to their various workstations. The men stuck to their schedules and were able to spend their free time however they wanted. But both women were employed at the center. That was a whole different story for them.

Suddenly Brock pounded the table with his palm. His grin widened. "Damn, it's good to have you here, Dent. Who'd have thought all three of us would have made it like this?"

Cole grinned. "Hey, we all survived. That's the most

important part. I'm happy to be alive and with whatever health and physical ability I have now. I know it'll get better—especially with Sandra at my side."

Denton had no one at his side, but he had his friends, and he hoped that, in time, their new partners would become his friends too. The three guys had all had girlfriends in the past and at no point had those relationships been allowed to break up the three men's friendships.

And instinctively he knew that these women wouldn't come between them either. Content in knowing that he had friends who would be there with him through thick and thin, a clan of like-minded people who would grow and develop as their relationships and families grew, he smiled.

He was truly blessed. Denton studied his friends' faces and nodded. "And I'm damn glad to be here too."

Chapter 5

F OR THE NEXT week and a half, Hannah went about her job but constantly noticed groups of people paired up in discussions, both professional and personal. Also, a lot of visitors came back and forth as several families checked out the facilities to see if it was the right place for their loved ones. Other family members came to visit loved ones. Everywhere Hannah looked, she saw togetherness. To combat being overwhelmed by her feelings, she focused on the people who were single at Hathaway. Shane and Stan came to mind, and there were certainly lots of others. Stan had a life downstairs with his own staff. She didn't know a whole lot about them. But as she gravitated away from the friend groups, she realized she was gravitating more toward people who were single.

As if singles would be more likely to become her friend, instead of trying to make friends with groups of people who were already linked together. She felt like she was on the outside, figuring out a way to get inside. That was wrong. It felt like high school all over again. She'd hated that time. She didn't want to fall into that same kind of mentality.

She walked to her office, sat down at her desk and worked through some patient files. Medical updates were to be entered manually into the computer. Bills needed to be processed, and there was always paperwork.

Dani walked in, a cup of coffee in hand, and sat down in Hannah's visitor chair. "Okay, so tell me what's wrong."

Hannah glanced at her in surprise. "What do you mean, *what's wrong?*"

"You," Dani said, her tone light. "The last few days you've been different."

Hannah winced. "Has it been that obvious?"

Dani nodded. "For someone who knows you and works with you every day, yes."

"Sorry. I've been thinking a lot about friends and friend groups and not having friends." She gave a weak half laugh. "The minute your mind picks up on a problem around you, all you see are the things that you don't have."

"Haven't you made friends here?" Dani asked carefully. "Everyone has lovely things to say about you and your performance."

Hannah smiled at her. "And that's all great because we also live here and work here. It's important that we also have a life that includes more than a working relationship. Friends are everywhere here. And I'm not one of them, it seems." She forced a smile. "Is anything wrong with me?" Dani's eyebrows rose in surprise, and Hannah quickly added, "I've been more introspective lately."

"There's nothing wrong with a little introspection at times," Dani said slowly, "but don't let it get carried away. I don't think there's anything wrong with you, Hannah. It may be that you're still fairly new here, and you're a hard worker who spends a lot of time on her job."

"I certainly understand that," Hannah said in relief. "Since I arrived at Hathaway House, I haven't taken the time to grow close to anybody else here." She smiled ruefully. "And that's probably not healthy either."

Dani nodded. "It does make sense that, if your entire life is wrapped up here, you should have other friends off the property or make friends here so that you can do things away from work. Just because you live here, it doesn't mean you have to be completely focused on this place."

"That's what I was thinking. But I don't know how to meet the people who do other things." She studied Dani. "And if I'm feeling that way, are others? Like, some of the patients maybe too?"

Dani glanced around the small office thoughtfully. "Maybe we need to organize more outings. For the ambulatory patients especially. Let's plan a social trip to town. See if we have a group of ten who we can take to the mall and out for lunch to the park ... maybe pick out a few sightseeing or shopping places that people want to go to."

"That's not a bad idea," Hannah agreed. "It might help to develop relationships for those patients who are isolated or only briefly get hugs. It can be lonely here," she admitted. "I hadn't realized how lonely I was until the last few days."

"Because of Denton's arrival?" Dani asked.

Hannah nodded. "And that's silly. Denton, Brock and Cole were friends long before they came here."

"True enough." Dani smiled. "And since you came here, we've also seen a surge in other relationships developing. Of which Aaron and I are a prime example. And the trend is continuing. Seeing that can make people want more than what they have."

"Exactly," Hannah said, deciding she'd whined enough. "A field trip next week sounds like fun."

Dani stood. "Put together a basic proposal. Give me some ideas of where and what people would like to do. Go talk to the ambulatory patients. We'll start with them.

Otherwise we'd have to bring a whole staffing crew with us to help out."

"Can do. But maybe we could do something modified for the less ambulatory patients. Just getting them out on the grounds, around the horses. And a picnic for them too. Regardless, how about I start small with the trip to town, and we'll see how it goes?"

"Sounds good. Let me know what you come up with." With that, Dani left Hannah's office. Surprisingly Hannah felt better. For the moment at least.

Notebook in hand, Hannah made her way to some of the patients, looking for suggestions and those wanting to participate in a field trip. When she got to Denton's room, she found him sitting slumped on his bed, his face flushed and sweaty.

She knocked and hesitantly stepped inside. "How are you, Denton? Looks like you've had a rough day so far."

He wiped his face with the towel in his hand. "I'm pretty tired," he admitted. "Who knew that recovery from an injury could be so harsh? In the military, we went through all kinds of physically strenuous exercise. We were constantly in training, constantly running, constantly doing feats. To be honest, it was harder than anything we'd ever done before." He shook his head. "There were times when I was taken to the edge of my endurance. My spirit was so low I felt I was done. That I was physically finished." He gave her a wan smile. "But I hit that point faster than I ever thought possible here."

She crossed her arms and stepped into his room. "Remember though, you are just starting out so don't be hard on yourself. What got you through those tough times in the military?" she asked curiously.

"My friends," he said. "Brock and Cole. They got me through the tough times. There was one time where I quit. I was done for. I knew I couldn't take one more step. They wouldn't listen to me. They grabbed me by the arms and dragged me forward. Because if I could take one more step on my own, then several more steps would help me get there. I let them help. That was a huge wakeup call for me. I was letting somebody else help me make my dreams happen. It's hard to admit when you need help. Yet, it's a great thing to understand that when you need help, somebody is there who cares." He collapsed backward on the bed and groaned. "Holy crap, I'm tired."

"Did you get lunch?" she asked.

He shook his head. "I'm trying to motivate myself to get something to eat. I need to. I'm really hungry, but I'm so tired."

"I'd suggest that you use the wheelchair, but I don't want to hurt your feelings."

He raised his head and looked at her. "If I could get into the wheelchair, I could probably help myself." He pushed himself into a sitting position, clearly wincing as he moved sore muscles. He glanced at the wheelchair and then at her. "Is it too late to eat?"

She glanced at her tablet. "It's one-thirty. You still have time." She walked to the wheelchair parked in the corner of his room and pushed it toward him. When it was right beside him, she said, "It's your choice."

He smiled and slowly made his way into the chair. Once he was seated, he collapsed and relaxed. "Lord, that feels better. Just the thought of forcing that leg and foot into any more exercise today is beyond me."

She hesitated. "Can you get yourself there, or would you

like me to help?"

"YOU KNOW? I'M so tired I won't be too proud to accept the offer of help." He inclined his head in her direction. "If you have a few moments, thank you. I could use a push."

She grinned. "It's nice to see you won't be stubborn."

He chuckled. "Oh, stubbornness I got in spades. The learning to give ... the wanting to accept ... remembering to be appreciative?" he said. "That's a talent."

She stepped behind the wheelchair and pushed him forward through the doorway. "Well, from what I can see, you got that talent down pat. I wish I did." Her voice had a serious tone to it.

He twisted to look up at her. "What do you mean?"

"I mean, you have the ability to make friends and keep friends. I was talking to Dani about it today. The three of you—Brock, Cole and you." She upped the wattage of her smile. "I, on the other hand, don't. Not real friends. Although if I had, would they become something I'd depend on now? I don't know."

He settled in as they rolled down the hallway toward the dining hall. "Something about being in BUD/s training instinctively let the three of us know that we had to help each other to make it through. It wasn't that anybody could make you run the miles when you wore down. You had to find that strength within yourself. But what about when you couldn't find it? That's when your friends pushed you, urging you to keep up, to dig deep. It helped knowing that you weren't alone. Knowing they were struggling too. It's hard when it looks like you're the only one who's not doing so well. The self-confidence takes a hit, and it's hard to recover from that."

"I can imagine," she said quietly. "You have a lot to be proud of in your life."

He nodded. "Just because my life went in a different direction, that doesn't mean it isn't full of good things."

She gave a light laugh that sounded false. "Maybe and maybe not. I can't see myself feeling terribly overjoyed by what I've accomplished so far."

"Particularly with friends, I gather?" He wanted to twist and look up at her again, but that was awkward and pretty hard on his back. But he could tell from the silence as she pushed him down the hallway and from the wheels silently spinning beneath them that he had hit the target. "I don't mean to hurt you," he said hesitantly. "I'm not sure that making friends is such a talent as much as it's the opportunity in accepting and taking up opportunities from crossing paths."

She stayed quiet, so he tried again.

"Meaning that it takes the right people at the right time under the right circumstances to click. And probably a lot of good people are here, and you're all doing the same things, but it can be a little easier to be friends and coworkers at the same time when you live here."

"Quite possibly." At that, she stopped at the large doorway. "Where do you want to sit?"

"Outside," he said. "Any chance I get, I like to be outside."

She pushed the wheelchair to the start of the buffet line.

He turned to look up at her. "Thanks for the assist." He gave her a big grin. Then seeing the uncertain look on her face, he asked in a gentle voice, "Have you eaten?"

She shoved her hands into the pockets of her long sweater and shook her head. "No, I guess time went by so fast this morning that I missed it," she confessed.

"In that case, this is one of those times where the right circumstances and the right people have come together, and they clicked." He grinned at her. "Come have lunch with me."

She hesitated, and he watched her inner struggle play out on her face. But then she stepped up behind him and said, "I might eat a little. I'm not terribly hungry." She grabbed two trays and put one in front of him and hers behind.

"You should eat. Particularly if you're worried about something. Stress is a killer on your stomach. Something I already know. I worried myself crazy for a long time and developed ulcers. Not fun."

"Normally I'm not a worrywart. But now, some of these self-revelations are a little harder to accept."

They stopped in front of the hot food. He couldn't see all the dishes, but he could read the labels on top.

"Let me help. What would you like?" she asked quickly.

It was Asian-fusion day. She efficiently filled his plate with a selection of foods that fit into his diet. They carried on past the others as she loaded up coffee and drinks for both of them. With the cutlery now on her tray, she looked around the room. "Left or right?"

He wondered, confused for a moment, then realized a pathway led to a set of tables on other side of the room. "The path of least resistance," he joked.

"That means right." She looked at his tray. "You ready to try this on your lap, or do you want me to take my tray and come back and get yours?"

A voice beside them piped up. "Not to worry, I'm right here," Dennis said. "I'll follow along with Denton's tray."

Together, the trio made their way to one of the larger tables sitting in the sun. Denton pulled up to the end where there were no chairs, and Dennis placed Denton's tray in front of him. They quickly removed everything off the tray and waited while Hannah unloaded hers. Then Dennis took the empty trays.

"Thank you, Dennis," both Denton and Hannah said in unison.

Denton lifted his face to the sun and closed his eyes. "This is simply wonderful," he murmured.

"We don't get that attitude very often in the first few days here," she said.

"That's too bad. People need to be more thankful for the simple things in life." He picked up his fork and speared a large piece of broccoli. He popped it into his mouth and smiled. "Perfect. Crunchy, fresh with a beautiful sauce." On that note, he dove into the rest of his meal. He watched as she picked her way through a much smaller portion of everything.

When he was halfway done, he motioned at her plate. "Eat up."

She glanced at him with a smile. "Isn't that my line?"

He chuckled. "Nobody's had to tell me to clean my plate since I was able to sit up on my own."

At that, she laughed out loud.

He was delighted to hear it. Her laughter was light and musical, turning heads and raining down across the deck. He doubted she had any idea how lovely she was. "You should do that more often."

She raised an eyebrow at him. "What? Laugh?"

He nodded. "Yes, exactly that." He gave her a wicked smile. "That sound lights up the whole room." And he picked up his fork and finished his meal.

Chapter 6

WHEN SHE FINISHED eating, Hannah pulled her coffee toward her, tucked her legs underneath her and settled back against the bench. She leaned one arm on the top of the railing and looked out over the pasture. "Dani's done such a beautiful job with this place."

"She has, indeed. I haven't gotten to meet the Major though. I understand he's quite a character."

She glanced at Denton, surprised. "Major hasn't come by to say hi?"

Denton shook his head. "But then again I haven't been here very long."

"True enough. He is quite a character, like everyone says."

"And the reason Dani started this place, right?" He looked up as if to assess Hannah's answer.

Hannah nodded. "Her father was an injured veteran and in rough shape. As he slowly improved, he and Dani created this business."

Denton raised his eyebrows. "Now that's having a passion and a purpose." He pushed away his empty plate and rubbed his tummy. "That feels a whole lot better."

She chuckled. "Nothing like good food to change your attitude."

"In this case, it was more about needing food to give me

some energy before I collapsed."

"Too much of a workout this morning?"

"I don't think so. Some days are better than others."

She studied him and realized he had no intention of saying more. He wasn't the kind to whine about something he couldn't change. He focused on what he could do, being appreciative of everything that was here and available for him. "I could learn a lot from you," she admitted. "You seem to have your priorities straight."

He shot her a piercing gaze. "So do you. You're here. You're helping people—that's huge."

"I don't have the skills I would like to have," she said, "and although I like this job and I like living here, it's been a little lonely."

He tilted his head to the side to watch her curiously. "And yet, you're surrounded by people."

"Back to that ... not sure I have what it takes to make good friends."

He shook his head. "You are really friendly. I haven't noticed anything odd in that way."

She chuckled. "How could you? You barely know me."

He lifted a finger and waggled it at her. "Not true. I've known you for what, ten days now?" He grinned. "In some parts of the world, that's long enough to get married."

At that, she laughed out loud again. "Well, I've never been married, so I wouldn't know."

He nodded. "Neither have I." That wicked grin flashed once more. "See? Now we've got all the preliminaries out of the way."

"You're incorrigible." She picked up her coffee cup, surprised to find her cheeks felt hot. Was she blushing? Was he flirting with her? How long had it been since she'd had a man do that? When she'd come here, she'd been happy to focus on helping others as she'd had such a hard time getting to know very many people at her old job. She had worked in a large legal firm, and it had been a lot of work with not a whole lot of time off, and all she'd done was return to her empty place and repeat the next morning. Here, her job was people more so than papers. And it was a good thing because it was making her a little more social, a little more comfortable in her own skin. And maybe that was the trick. She'd been intimidated at the law office. She'd done her best, but when she'd seen this job advertised, she had applied and had no trouble walking away from the other one.

She'd been here a year, and although she certainly didn't feel the way she had before, she hadn't warmed up to others and quickly found the group of friends that she'd secretly hoped for. And yet, she knew that was her fault. When her shifts were done, she ate—usually alone, sometimes with others—and then went to her room. She went for a lot of solo walks and drove by herself into town on a regular basis, but she hadn't reached out either. She hadn't asked any of the staff to accompany her on those excursions. She was always friendly but never a friend.

"Heavy thoughts?"

She raised her head to meet his gaze and smiled. "Just a further realization that, although I've been friendly, I haven't been terribly welcoming or inviting of others into my life."

"Maybe that's a good thing," he said. "It takes time to settle in, and it takes time to trust those around us. To know who they are. Don't settle into a new place too quickly or jump in to make friends right away. Sometimes it's better to understand who they all are and decide which ones you want to make friends with first."

"Oh, I've done that. But sadly it's time to stretch a little more."

"So why not go around and ask people if they want to ride to town with you and what they like to do?"

She studied his face suspiciously, but he seemed genuinely curious. "We're organizing a trip to town for the more mobile patients," she said. "Depending on where and what people would like to do, we'll run several such trips. For people who like to go shopping we will do a trip to the mall. Some people might want to get out and do something at the parks if that's possible."

"Although I have challenges, I wouldn't mind seeing more of the area. A day trip sounds great."

She smiled. "I'll put your name down on the list then, pending your medical team's approval. What is it you'd like to do? Go for a drive to get away, or do you need to go shopping for something in particular?"

He frowned. "I don't think I have anything I *need* to do. Although, if a bank is close by, I could use an ATM machine."

"Okay." She nodded. "I'll let you know what days we set up and which places we'll go to." She stood. "Do you need a hand back to your room?" She picked up their two coffee cups and waited for his answer.

He shook his head. "I have another fifteen minutes until my session with the doctor this afternoon. I think I'll stay right here and enjoy the sun a little while longer."

She held up his coffee cup. "You want a refill?"

He glanced at it and shook his head. "Nope, thanks. I'll sit here, relax, close my eyes, and I'll take my time getting back to my room." He glanced at her. "But thank you for your help."

She shrugged. "Anytime." She walked back inside and deposited the dirty cups on the appropriate cart.

Dennis winked at her. "Is this another shipboard romance happening?"

She shook her head. "Not likely."

He studied her intently for a long moment. "Not so sure about that. Looks to me like a nice pairing."

She flushed again, made her excuses and hurried off to her office. His chuckle followed. She winced. The last thing she wanted was for anyone to know how much she liked Denton. But apparently, it was already obvious.

Inside though, the thought of a romance between the two of them was enough to make her heart smile. Nothing would come of it, of course, but that didn't mean she couldn't enjoy the moment.

Then she'd need to move back to reality—and fast.

DENTON WAS LUCKY. Luckier than he thought. So many things came easily for him. But talking with Hannah made him realize that, for some people, making friends was hard. She appeared to be a lovely person. But friendships developed over time. Good friends were there through the hard times, not just the good times. Of course, the BUD/s training had brought him and Brock and Cole together. It was the worst time of his life, but it was also one of the best. And if someone didn't have an experience like that in their life, with people at their side, Denton could imagine it would be hard to bond at that level. He also had to remember that, just because he had friends here, the work was still his to do. His friends would be there to cheer him, but Denton was the one who had to take those steps.

He was the one who had to do the work and to show the progress. He was the one who had to go from point A to point B, and if he didn't make it, it was all on him. And that was one thing he knew he avoided really looking at. He was trying hard to be here, trying hard to do whatever needed to be done, but there was a lot of pressure. It wasn't that they used the pressure to make him advance—it was pressure he was putting on himself. It didn't have to be that way. But he didn't want to be less of a success story than his friends were. He didn't want them to look at him and point out his performance. He didn't want to lose their respect because he fell and gave up.

Was he worrying too much about their opinion? They were friends but still ... he'd always been his own man. At least in his head, but things were different here ... he hated the feeling but insecurity ate at him. And he found himself questioning everything he did.

That was something about having friends. You wanted them to admire what you'd done. You wanted them to feel proud of you. But when they didn't feel proud of you, you also needed them to get in your face and say, *Buck up and go on. No room here for slackers.*

If recovery had taught him one thing, it was that a whole group of people in rehab gave up early on. These people said the work was too much. They achieved a certain level of health, and that was okay. It was an acceptable level for them, and then they didn't try anymore. Because the rest of it was hard. It was *really* hard. The pain was incredible for the level of physicality that they were expected to do.

The delving into psychological issues and fears was equally as hard. And he knew that bothered him the most.

He'd barely even touched the surface with his group counselor. Denton had so much to be grateful for that he got impatient at himself for being so afraid. Even if it was natural. As if he expected to be above that. Unlike a lot of people, he didn't have a network of business associates ready to offer him jobs or money. He didn't have a wife to go home to or children who didn't care what kind of shape he was in, yet were simply happy that he came home.

He was alone. His mother had passed away a few years back. His friends were here, but they also had their own lives. And for the first time, Denton realized that with them having partners, those relationships could easily end up in marriage. His friends could end up developing families and different lives away from him. He'd never considered that.

Even while they were all doing their military thing, Denton knew there was a possibility of all of them going in opposite directions once they left the military. But that was sometime out in the distant future. When it came sooner than expected and in an unlikely way, they all were doing their best to get back on their feet, and automatically that meant getting back together again. That they came together to heal was huge. But as they healed, the faster they moved on with their individual lives. The others were moving at a faster rate than Denton was. But it wasn't the rate that bothered him. It was the fact that, as they moved on, they might move far away.

People had a lot more opportunities to maintain friendships over long distances because of the Internet, but it wasn't the same as having the guys right next door—barbecues in the backyard, slinging beer on a Friday night, closing the day down.

Denton was tired, but he still had to return to his room

to deal with the next item on his schedule.

He needed his appointment with the shrink today. She appeared to be very knowledgeable and very intuitive. Almost too intuitive. He slowly made his way to his room. This session would be in his room, and that was a darn good thing. The only good thing about the whole appointment was being able to get out of the chair and up onto the bed, maybe even put a blanket over his legs. He already felt chilled now because he knew the next session would be hard emotionally.

It was also hard to rip yourself apart, figuring out what was wrong on the inside and what was stopping you from being the best you could be in handling all the things thrown at you. You had to get away from the guilt of getting injured and to stop playing the blame game—both difficult to walk away from.

Why had it been him? Why hadn't it been someone else? Why had he been the one in the unit assigned to this post? Why had he been asked to drive that truck? And the blame just continued. He hadn't thought he held very much of that inside. But the more his therapist dug in, the more she prodded, and the more she poked, he realized that, indeed, although he may not have had much of his anger visible, he still held a lot of it inside. He knew it was also necessary to get rid of it, but purging one's soul was darn hard.

He was grateful when he got to his room and realized the psychologist hadn't arrived yet. He made his way to the side of the bed, and using the bed for support, he slowly stood up, again hating the shakiness of his limbs. He sat down, shuffled his butt until he was leaning against the headboard and pulled up the blanket from the end of the bed over his legs. As he studied his damaged calf, a tremor rippled up and down the muscles. He pulled the calf toward him and gently massaged it. He had a cream the therapist had given him. He opened that tube, put some cream on his fingers and slowly worked it deep into the muscle. He knew it was better than before, but it was hard to see any improvement from ten days ago.

In fact, the improvements were all about pain. He was digging deeper, and that was an improvement. He was pushing himself harder, and that was an improvement. But he wasn't seeing the results he wanted to see. He was becoming impatient. After a ton of hard work and time, he wanted to see the results. And he understood in his own mind how hard Brock must have worked because Denton had seen how Brock had been right after his accident.

Brock had been flat on his back and in terrible shape. To see the man now, well, there was absolutely zero comparison. The same for Cole. Denton understood a lot about what had happened to Cole when he'd first arrived. He had teased him about it gently because Cole had always felt like he was playing catch-up. Denton hadn't felt the same way. But in one way, he did understand Cole's competitiveness, Cole's need to prove himself in light of Brock's rehab success.

Raised with little money, and often with government subsidies or charity, Denton always had a sense of *I don't deserve this. People are doing this because I'm injured.* It was the same as when he was growing up—people would be nice to him because his mother was poor, and his life must, therefore, really suck. It was hard to argue with that logic.

But this left an underlying fear that he hadn't gotten anywhere on his own. Case in point, like it had taken others to get him here to Hathaway House.

A lot of things about his life hadn't been easy. But he

had loved his mom. They'd been very close. The two of them had as much fun as any father, mother and son combination could have, but no doubt, there had been hard times. It was difficult to see other families operate in a typically normal way versus what he had experienced. When she'd died, he'd turned to Brock and Cole. And they'd been there for him.

As he lay here, tired, worn out and with a full tummy, he heard a knock at the door. He rolled his head to the side and smiled when he saw Dr. Hutchinson. "Good afternoon, Doc."

She smiled and waved at him. "Considering you're in bed, maybe I should say *good evening*. Are you ready to sleep? Had a tough morning?"

Her gaze was intense, and he knew her eyes understood so much more than he would like. That was one thing about the people here—it didn't matter which staff member was helping him, it was like they all could see into his soul.

"I am more tired than usual." He stretched out his bad leg, closed the tube of cream and pulled the blanket back over it. "That doesn't mean I don't have enough energy to talk with you though."

She chuckled. "Our sessions don't always have to be difficult."

"So you say," he said, knowing he sounded slightly cynical. "But it hasn't exactly been easy so far."

"It's not like you're in tears and angry about any of it."

He shrugged. "What good would that do?"

She nodded, then pulled up a chair and sat down beside him. "So, tell me the truth. How do you feel about being here?"

He had to think about it for a long moment, and then

he was as honest as he could be. "I'm very pleased to be here."

"Would you have gotten the same care, the same advantages, the same improvements elsewhere?"

He nodded. "Quite likely I could have. But here I have the added benefit of having both my buddies with me."

"How does that make you feel?"

He smiled. "Loved, secure, happy and grounded."

And damned if she didn't come at him with another dozen questions. He did his best to answer everything. As he'd found out with her, every time they had a session, a little bit more of himself was revealed. Sometimes that was good, sometimes bad.

"Do you feel that your friends are responsible for your improvement?"

He shook his head. "No. They created their milestones ahead of me, and they're cheerleaders, but when the work is there in front of me, only one person has to do it, and that's me. They have their own work to look after. It's up to me to deal with mine."

"Good answer. Have you made any attempt to meet new friends?"

He frowned at her. "You asked that last time, and I thought it odd then too."

She shrugged. "I need to know that you aren't closing yourself off from other people. You came here with the expectation of having friends already in place, and often we find that means people aren't open to making new connections."

Her words somewhat echoed Hannah's earlier comment, and he settled back and considered that. "I'd like to think I am open to making new friends. But you may be right. I came knowing I had friends and a friend group already in place, and I didn't worry about anything else."

"And you think that's good for you?"

He shrugged. "I don't know what's good for me anymore. And I can only handle so many self-improvement things on a day-to-day basis, and if that's not one of them, then that's not one of them. I have to do what's best for me right now, not what might be good for other people." He studied her carefully. "Has anybody complained that I've been unfriendly?"

"I have no idea," she said. "I haven't heard any. I wondered if you were feeling open to making new friends or if you feel you're complete with the two you have."

He shifted uncomfortably on the bed. Once again Hannah's face and her comment about having difficulty making friends rose to the forefront. "I don't know," he said, his tone short.

"Well, think about it over the next few days, and let me know if anything comes to mind." She checked her watch. "I'm afraid we'll have a short session today. I have to deal with a couple patients coming and going."

He hated that his insides jumped for joy. He hoped it wasn't something he had said or one of his answers. Because it would make him feel like he needed to work on something else. What he wanted was to relax and not work on anything. He wanted to have a normal day.

She stood. "I understand they are arranging some trips into town. Are you interested in going?"

"Hannah already signed me up." He waited, wondering if that was all she would ask. But she smiled and nodded and wrote something down on her tablet that worried him. She made her way to the door.

He couldn't help himself. "What did you just write down?"

She raised an eyebrow. "A note about you wanting to go into town." She gave him a brighter smile and then left.

And for the first time in a long time, he wasn't sure he believed her.

He hated the worry, the doubts. That was one thing about his medical team. They were here for him, but at the same time, he wanted to know what they saw when they looked at him.

He thought he was doing fine—or was he deluding himself?

Chapter 7

I F HANNAH HAD known how much fun it would be setting up trips to town, she would have proposed the idea ages ago. Over the next few days she found herself enjoying having the chance to talk to all the different patients, to see what it was they were looking for in an outing—to shop and to visit people. Some wanted to get out because the walls were closing in on them, and they needed a change of scenery. Some had brought up activities, like bowling or seeing a movie. Several wanted to go to the mall because they needed clothing or stuff that they hadn't had a chance to pick up themselves, and others needed to replenish personal hygiene items. She made extensive notes, then a couple days later met with Dani. She sat down in the visitor's chair and smiled at her boss.

"That was fun and a little frustrating."

Dani's grin widened, and she leaned back in her chair.

"We have fourteen requests to go to town. Of those, ten would like to go on the first trip, if possible."

"Well, we were looking for ten. So that works."

"Sure, but none of them agree on what they want to do. One wants to see a movie. Another wants to visit the dentist." Hannah raised her eyebrows as she glanced over at Dani. "Never even occurred to me that somebody here might need to go to the dentist, but of course, you don't have a dentist or hygienist coming here, do you?"

Dani chuckled. "Nope, we sure don't. We arrange for the dentist or optometrist trips as required. Some must go in for the prosthetic engineering, et cetera. We set these visits up all the time. But I'm not sure that should be part of a social outing."

Hannah agreed. "Several want to go shopping. Some need shaving gear. Some need a couple more T-shirts, underwear, socks—that type of thing. Everybody was excited at the idea of getting out."

"Good. So, if we remove the one who needs to go to the dentist—I'll make arrangements for him on his own—that leaves nine, correct?"

"Yes, but I'm thinking Roger might still want to go out for the day. A dental trip can be handled separately, but I don't think he should come off the list."

"Okay, we can take ten but half that would be better. We also wanted to keep this as a fun social trip, not for shopping, but might manage to combine it. We'll have the driver and some other staff, depending on the ambulatory level of those going," she said. "Let me see the list."

Hannah handed over the sheet of paper.

Dani took a few moments to peruse it. "These people are all good candidates for this field trip. Every one of them can handle their own wheelchair or crutches. They are all ambulatory. We will go to a park if that's what they want. We can even arrange to have either a picnic with food from the kitchen or we can pick up food in town and take it to the park."

"What about the movie?"

Dani shrugged. "We can certainly drop off some people at the movie theater, but it would have to be a matinee, and

while they are at the movie, the others could be shopping."
She glanced up at Hannah. "See if you can get the movie-
goers to agree on a movie at the Theodore."

"Also several of the patients asked who was paying for
this."

Dani glanced up and frowned. "The center will absorb
the cost of the gas, the driver, lunch if it's a picnic basket
from here and providing the staff. But the individual patients
will be required to look after things like their own movie
theater tickets and their shopping purchases and if we choose
lunch out."

"Okay, that's more than fair. That'll make several of
them quite happy."

Dani gave her a sharp look. "Are you hearing any concerns about money from anybody?"

Hannah sat back and thought for a moment. "I think a
couple people were grumbling a bit about not having
enough. But in this case, I would be a little more concerned
if people didn't have the money to get things like socks and
underwear," she confessed.

After talking with Dani, Hannah took her notes back to
her desk. One of the best things about this job was the
variety of the tasks she got to do. And the people she had a
chance to work with. The atmosphere here was different.
Sometimes it was sober, sometimes it was a delight. Everybody cheered and joined in each other's personal successes.
But it was equally hard when there were difficulties. There
had been quite a kerfuffle when Cole had had to go back to
the hospital. There was a lot of soul-searching going on in
the staff meetings, to see if they could've done something
better.

So far, she'd been blessed to see so many people improve

to the point of leaving and to watch new people arrive. There was nothing quite like watching the progress of someone doing something as simple as getting a cup of coffee. They struggled in the beginning and within a few months had no problems whatsoever. Attitude, physical ability and perception of their life completely changed in a short period of time.

Of course that brought her mind right around to Denton again. She decided to sweep through the dining hall and get a coffee rather than any of the other spots in the building that housed coffeemakers. She knew she wasn't fooling anyone, least of all herself.

If he just so happened to be there, she could walk over to say hi. And it would give her a chance to talk to him about the outing as planned. She thought he would like to go no matter what the trip entailed. She well understood the need to get out once in a while—to see something different, do something out of the routine. She just had to see if his medical team approved this day trip.

She entered the dining hall, her notepad tucked under her arm, and headed toward the coffee bar. Her cup poured, she stood there for a long moment, and then surveyed the space.

Dennis was there, cleaning tables. She smiled at him. "How's your day going, Dennis?"

He looked up and beamed a smile at her. "It's going great. How about you?"

She nodded. "It's good. It's one thing about being here—most of the days are good."

He nodded and laughed. "There are a lot of good things about this place. But that sense of hope and achievement, those are hard to beat. We are lucky enough to get the benefit of everybody else's hard work." He shook his head as he walked past. "It's hard to not feel proud when seeing so many other people achieve things in their lives."

Hannah carried her coffee out to the deck and stood for a moment, letting the sun bathe her face. Dennis was right. Being here was a hell of an achievement, and she was lucky to witness all of the patients' successes. As she turned to head back to her office, she saw Denton making his way on his crutches toward Dennis. There was a short conversation, and then Dennis quickly disappeared into the back. She wondered what was up.

Denton made his way to the closest table and sat down heavy and hard. He looked completely wiped out. Immediately she headed for him. "Denton, are you okay?" She didn't mean to sound so worried, but she was.

The look on his face was just awful.

DENTON GAVE HER a brief smile. "I'm fine, but my blood sugar's completely wiped out. I tell you, there are days when I have to wonder if I am diabetic."

"Have you been tested?"

He nodded. "I have a super high metabolism and have to watch the balance of sugars versus proteins. Dennis is getting me some food." He gave her a boyish smile that was more cheerful than the first one he'd attempted. "The good news is, I get to eat a lot."

That moment Dennis came back with a tray he placed in front of Denton. The plate was filled with an assortment of fresh fruit and nuts.

"Not bad ... protein, fats, carbs and fruit for easy sugar," she said, studying his snack.

"Exactly." He lifted the fork, and she was amazed to see how much of an effort it appeared to be for him. A tremor ran through his hand as he took several bites.

She figured it would probably take ten to fifteen minutes before his system realized food was coming. She pulled out a chair. "Would you mind company?"

He waved at her. "Please, sit. I'm so sorry. I should've invited you to join me. My manners now are nonexistent."

She chuckled softly. "You have a lot more things to worry about than your manners." She watched him eat for a minute. "How about I get you a cup of coffee to go with that?"

He glanced at her, and his face broke into a grateful smile. "Thank you. But I can get it myself. You know you don't have to wait on me, right?"

She shook her head, rose and brought over the coffee. "Sometimes it's nice to help people."

He was obviously feeling better because his grin deepened. "Besides, that's what friends do."

She chuckled, remembering their early discussion. "Absolutely."

He polished off his food and pushed back his plate with a happy sigh. "Now that's a whole lot better."

"Does this happen a lot?"

He shook his head. "I didn't have enough for breakfast. My mistake. I won't do that again."

She nodded, watching him carefully as the color returned to his face, and the absolute sheer fatigue slipped off his features. "It's amazing how quickly that helped."

"I'll be back to normal within another few minutes." He studied her for a long moment. "You know? I have been thinking a lot about the discussion we had the other day. About friends. I realized there's one thing that you do very well that I need to learn to do."

She looked at him in surprise. "What's that?"

"Stand on my own two feet when I need to—without friends to support me."

Chapter 8

HANNAH STARED AT him in surprise. "Why is that an issue?"

He toyed with his coffee cup for a long moment before he looked at her and gave her the ghost of a smile. "Well, Brock is leaving in only two to three weeks or so. But only because I was talking to you did I consider it. One of the reasons I was so excited to come here was because my friends were here. Friends who have always been part of my adult life, helping me get through the tough times. Not sure I would have gotten through it without them."

She sat back. "I'm sure you could have," she said warmly.

"But I don't *know* that I could," he said with a gentle smile. "It's not been something I've ever had to do. It's not that I've ever been tested to be sure."

"What about growing up?"

He shrugged. "A rural high school and elementary school was normal." He chuckled. "I know I had friends. It's one of the reasons why, when I was at BUD/s training, it was easy for me to sort through and pick out people who I knew were my kind. And teamwork has always been a big part of military life. Particularly in my case. Our unit was tight. We are brothers, and we always had each other's back. And that hasn't changed, even though the three of us are out of the navy now. That we're all injured and that we're all here adds to the fact that we're helping each other."

"Are you afraid that if Brock and Cole weren't here, you wouldn't do as well?"

He winced, then nodded. "Maybe a little."

She tilted her head and considered the issue. "For myself, I've always been mostly alone. I kept trying to look for people who were of my mind-set, but I never really succeeded."

"I keep coming back to a fundamental question. If I had been injured first and if I'd have come here alone, would I have done as well as Brock?"

She stared at him, seeing the earnestness, the determination, the absolute knowledge that he'd had a helping hand when Brock didn't. And the worry that Denton couldn't have done as well on his own.

"I don't know, but I believe you would have. It's not that you had friends to help you do the actual rehab here, but they were a kind of a security blanket, knowing that, if you ever needed somebody to call on or someone to talk to, they were there."

"Absolutely. But Brock had to do it himself. Brock had to stand on his own two feet to make this happen. Cole came in, and he was so busy playing catch-up with Brock he almost lost his way. But because Brock was here and the others were here to help Cole slow down and to give him a chance to be here on his own, he picked up and is doing well. But now I've arrived, and of course, already this whole group was here waiting for me, like a safety net. That made it easier on me."

"What's wrong with that?" she exclaimed. "This isn't meant to be a battle of the toughest or a test for the best-mental-fitness-single-performance. Every one of you has different challenges and issues to overcome. It's not been easy for anybody."

He settled back, staring at his coffee.

She leaned forward and gently placed her hand on top of his. "I'm so sorry if I made you doubt yourself. That's not what I intended at all."

His gaze lifted, and he studied her. "You had nothing to do with me doubting myself. I think a part of me says I'm not as good as the other two because this wasn't easier for me."

She shook her head. "Why does any of this matter? This is hard enough for all of you." She glared at him. "If you need to have some kind of a test to see how you do without your friends, pick something that doesn't matter quite so much. This is when you *need* your friends. Be grateful you have them."

"I am grateful," he said sincerely. "Don't get me wrong. It makes me wonder how I would fare on my own. It's not that I'm being competitive because I'm not."

It never occurred to her that he would question such a thing. She'd been alone so much of her life, looking on the outside of all these groups, wondering how to become part of them, and instead he was inside one of the groups, wondering if he could stand without support from that same group. She shook her head. "I can't say it's anything I ever wondered about."

"That's because you have yourself. When things get down, you know you can buck up."

"So can you." She leaned forward earnestly. "More than most people. You did what was necessary—you made it. And now you're lucky enough to have friends on your side to help you get through another difficulty. Don't ever doubt that you're incapable of doing it on your own."

He gave her a sheepish grin and nodded. "Maybe you're right. But it started eating away at me today, thinking that I've always had help, that someone was always there, giving me assistance. Just even being here," he said. "I didn't have money and the financial backing." He lifted his arms and opened them wide. "Why me? Because I have friends? Because I know people?"

She shook her head. "Because you're in need." She grinned. "Talk to Dani about that one. She has several people on tap who she contacts on a regular basis when she sees people in need who don't have the funds to come to Hathaway. She has a rotating system. She always has somebody who cannot pay the full price. Does that make a difference to her? Not at all. Should it make a difference to you? Absolutely not."

He leaned forward. "That's what I mean. See? I couldn't get here on my own. It took her. It took her financial backers to get me here, whoever they were."

She opened her mouth and then closed it. "I think you're going about this from a completely skewed perspective. It's not that you're not grateful for all you've been given, but you're questioning whether you deserve any of this. There are so many other things you could sit here and question. This doesn't need to be one of them. When you get a gift like financial backing, it should have you thinking of how best you can make them not regret giving it to you."

Denton sat there and stared at her, a huge smile building on his face. "You know? That was a promise I made to myself when I got here—to do a damn good job of everything for everyone who had done something to get me here," he said. "Somewhere along the line, I had forgotten that promise."

She smiled. "It doesn't need to be brought up every moment of the day. Every day it's a challenge to step up and do what you can do. It's doing and knowing that you've done your best, day after day, that counts. And that is hard to do. Hard to maintain."

He chuckled. "You'd make a hell of a cheerleader."

"I was never a cheerleader. I never made the team." She sat back in her chair. "I was always average at a lot of things but never great at anything."

His eyebrows shot up. "The one thing you are not is average," he said. He reached across the table this time and cupped her hand with his. His strong fingers closed gently around her much smaller hand. "You are very special."

She wanted to withdraw her hand, but he wouldn't let her.

He continued quietly. "And you're not used to compliments. You're not used to people saying good things about you because you're not used to having friends."

She tilted her head to the side. "Most of the friends I thought I once had used to insult each other rather than compliment them," she said, attempting to keep her voice light rather than share that pain. She loved the feel of his much rougher skin against hers. They were just so different. His hand was strong, lean and masculine—hers was softer, rounder, slim. And so very feminine in comparison. She stared at their joined hands, spreading her fingers out to line up with his. "You're right. I'm not used to compliments. That makes me feel socially awkward."

"You're not socially awkward. You're a very good person on the inside, so maybe you're one of those people who likes to have one or two good friends instead of a whole pile of acquaintances."

She nodded. "The one good friend I had died. Way back when I was twelve. She died in a car accident with her mom." She bit her lip at the memory. "It was hard for me, but my parents ... I don't think they understood how absolutely destroyed I was."

"Was that your first experience with death?"

She nodded. "It was. And it was a hell of a lesson."

He gave her a gentle, knowing smile. "Maybe it's time for you to examine that. Because what we tend to learn from our first major tragedy is an awareness that people do disappear forever. People who we love and care about from one moment to the next are gone. And a lot of people close off their feelings because they think if they care again and lose that person too, it would be devastating. I've seen this happen time and time again," he said. "They choose not to have good friends to save themselves the pain of losing them in the future."

She sat back and stared at him. "You know? I had totally forgotten about that accident. It was so long ago." She cast her mind back and winced. "In fact, I'd even changed schools around that time. I couldn't stand being around the same people and the same places, the school breaks and recesses I'd spent with her. I figured, in a new school, I would have new experiences, new friends, but I was still so hurt and in so much pain I closed myself off."

He nodded in a slow, compassionate way. "Chances are that's what this is all about. Open yourself up to a little bit of trust in your life, and you'll be just fine."

She chuckled. "I don't think it's quite that easy."

"Why don't we put it to the test over the next few days?"

he suggested. "We work hard at me standing on my own two feet without always thinking about my friends, and you doing something every day to make new ones."

She chuckled. "Well, that's easier on me probably."

"The people you have to pick from are all around you, but that doesn't mean you want to make friends with all of them." He waggled his eyebrows at her. "So, what do you think?"

She held out her hand to shake on it. "Sure. But you'd better take good care of yourself because if I find you lapsing, forgetting food throughout the day, then I win," she said with a mild threat.

His grin widened. "Deal."

THERE WAS NO reason for Denton to be bothered about his friendships, but at the same time, they did concern him. Because as his friends headed off into their futures, on their own paths, Denton was afraid the shock of losing them both would be a bit much. It wouldn't be at the same time so he'd have a chance to adjust to the loss but ... He hated to think that that would even come into question because he wanted them to be happy. It didn't mean they would necessarily separate, but their relationships would change.

Hannah was right about something else. He'd allowed his blood sugar to drop, weakening him. That shouldn't have happened. Normally he kept snacks with him all the time to pick up his energy level. It had something to do with his muscles dumping the glycogen after working out way too fast. He didn't quite understand it. But he knew that if he didn't take care of himself, his blood sugar levels would drop.

He had a full afternoon ahead. It was the mental stuff that was rough, but he was determined to do as good a job as he could. He pushed himself away from the table and slowly positioned his crutches under his arms, noting his legs were not quite so shaky, and headed toward his room. Once there, he realized he was still feeling the fatigue. Normally it wouldn't come back this fast. But then again, he'd wiped himself out. The workout this morning had been brutal. He probably shouldn't have been on the crutches but in his wheelchair. And he also hadn't had a chance to get to his massage after his physiotherapy session because Shane had been called away.

In this weak moment, he was forced to face the psychologist. That would have scared any man who didn't want to talk about his feelings as much as the shrinks wanted them to. He knew he would do just fine with his life. So what if he was missing his little toe from his left foot and the bulk of his hamstrings on his right leg? His back was a bit more of an issue, but he'd come a long way just to get to this point. His medical team had worked magic. And being here had mentally worked magic too.

There was a knock at the door, and he looked up to see Shane.

The physio walked into his room. "I heard you crashed."

Denton nodded. "Nothing to worry about. I'm prone to swinging blood sugar levels. I did too much this morning and didn't have a snack." Shane opened his mouth, but Denton held up a hand. "I know you told me to make sure I grabbed something. But I think I got lost on my phone for a bit and didn't have time."

Shane fisted his hands on his hips and glared at him in mock anger. "Well, that'll be the last time I'll let you get away with that."

Denton rolled his eyes and grinned. He knew Shane cared. And that was one of the things that made this place so special. "Don't worry. It's the last time I'll do it too." He shuffled back on the bed where he could lay against the headboard. "Also I'm paying for it because I didn't get a massage."

"How is your schedule this afternoon? Do you want to do that now?"

"I have a visit with Dr. Hutchinson about now." He leaned across the bed, pulled his tablet toward him and studied his schedule. "Yes, that's next. I also have a checkup with the doctor this afternoon as well, but after that, I would be free." He lifted his head to look at Shane. "Unless that doesn't work for you?"

Shane scrolled through his own tablet. "I'll be back before four. You could have a good massage and then dinner."

"Unless I fall asleep and sleep through dinner." He chuckled. "I have to admit, I'm pretty tired." He watched as Shane made several notes. "I don't think I overdid it badly today. I think it was the combination of the blood sugar and the workout," he rushed to say. "The workout wasn't too hard. It was just the combination."

Shane nodded. "Still, we'll adjust your schedule to make sure you get your snack and see how that works going forward."

With that, he took his leave. As he walked out, the psychologist walked in. They spoke in the doorway for a couple minutes. Denton wondered if they were discussing him, but it wasn't for him to worry about.

He had enough in his life to worry about without adding to it.

He didn't want his friends to know about his worries either. He didn't want them to be hurt by his fear he couldn't stand up without them, but he knew that if they heard the discussion, they'd probably feel exactly that. He pasted on a smile as the doctor walked in.

She pulled up a chair. "I'm pretty sure we met like this the other day too."

He gave her a half laugh. "This time it was due to my own stupidity."

She nodded. "Then tell me about it."

Chapter 9

THE FIRST SOCIAL trip, minus Denton, went off without a hitch, making it a twice-monthly event to the delight of everyone. For the next several days, Hannah focused on being a little friendlier to a few more people around her. She felt uncomfortable picking one person, so she decided she should be friendlier with everyone. She could work with that. She overheard a couple people saying she was in a much better mood these days, and they were wondering what was going on. Of course, she'd already heard her name linked with Denton's, and that bothered her. When she stopped to check in with him on the fourth day, she brought up her concerns.

"I don't know if my attempts are working or not."

"It's not something you can ask about or quantify," Denton replied. "It's something we have to judge for ourselves."

She shrugged. "But I'm trying to be much friendlier."

He stopped and looked at her. He put down the towel he'd been folding among the clothes he'd been putting away when she came in. "You can't just be friendlier. Because they don't realize you're purposefully being friendlier to them but think you're simply happier in general." He returned to folding his clothes, thankfully not seeing the color rise on her cheeks. "This can always be something situational. You have to pick out one person, maybe one person per day, and do something very friendly for them."

"Well, that hardly seems fair. Isn't it better if I'm friendlier with everyone, rather than picking and choosing individual people?"

"But then you don't possibly hurt people, and you don't chance getting hurt if they don't pick you back."

She stared at him. "Oh, my God. That's what I'm doing, right?"

He walked over carefully, on his own steam, and he gave her hand a squeeze, then stepped back. "Maybe. But that doesn't make it wrong. It's a learning process. You have to open yourself up to them, the same as you're hoping they will to you."

She nodded slowly. "Well, so far I think I've failed then." She shook her head. "I thought this would be easy. So, enough about me. What about you? How did you do for the last few days?"

"I've been so damn busy," he said, now sitting on the side of the bed. "Between one meeting and appointment and another, it's been easier to not think about my friends."

"And how are you feeling about that?" she asked. "How do you rely less on your friends but not have them feel like you're cutting them out of your life?"

He stared at her and raised an eyebrow. "Now that's a damn good question. Just because I'm being independent doesn't mean I make them feel like I don't want them around." They exchanged sad smiles.

"It's not quite as easy as you thought, is it?" she asked.

He shook his head as his phone buzzed. He pulled it out and studied the screen. "It's Brock. He says he hasn't seen me in a few days."

She nodded. "That would be your cue. Have coffee with them. See how you feel. See how your response is to see him. He's contacted you independently, and you're feeling more independent and self-sufficient. Then go meet him on equal terms. If you're approaching this from a perspective of feeling needy, then wait a little longer until you feel more grounded and prefer standing on your own feet."

He stared at her for a moment. "It didn't take you long to pick that up."

She chuckled. "I suggest we check back in a couple more days."

"Sure … but does that mean we don't get to see each other for a couple mornings?"

She spun around, knowing that the tingle in her cheeks meant she had turned bright pink. She hoped her voice didn't sound too girlish. "Absolutely not. We could do coffee sometime even?"

He shook his head. "I'd like that. Inside or outside, that would be lovely."

Hannah smiled from ear to ear. "Good, let's try for that soon." Not believing she'd flirted with him, she hurried out. She pressed her hands to her cheeks as she rushed down the hallway, feeling the heat in her palms. She prayed she wouldn't run into anybody who would do nothing but raise eyebrows and ask questions she had no intention of answering. She dashed into her office and plunked herself down at her desk.

Somehow that relationship had moved from the casual level up to the level of a special friend. She couldn't be happier. Then she remembered how she'd kept herself separate over the years to avoid being hurt. She'd missed out on opportunities like these. She definitely needed to branch out in finding friends. Who interested her? Who did she want to be friendlier with? She really liked Dani. She liked Sandra. And well, if she was getting together with Denton, there were always his friends, Brock and Cole. That thought felt a bit tenuous. How could she make friends with Denton's friends on the off chance she and Denton had made a connection? She pushed that thought from her mind and focused on her work.

Several hours later Hannah glanced at the clock and realized the lunch hour was almost over. She wasn't terribly hungry, but she could use a coffee break. And some fresh air would absolutely help. She picked up her coffee cup and wandered into the dining hall. There she filled up her mug and turned to see Dennis.

"You didn't eat lunch today?" he asked.

She smiled up at him as she was reminded what a nice man he was. "With all the people around here, how could you possibly notice I didn't come in and eat?" she teased.

His grin was wide and happy. "I always keep track of my favorite people," he announced. "And you don't eat enough."

"That's not fair," she protested. "I eat very well."

He motioned toward the buffet table. "I was about to pack it away. Can I get you something?"

She stopped and looked at what was offered. "The Greek salad looks so lovely."

"Well, it was lovelier when I first put it out there. Right now it's looking a little sad. I can freshen it with a little more cheese though." He walked away and returned with a bowl of Greek salad topped with more feta cheese. He put it on a tray and pulled out a plate. "Let's see what we have to go with it."

She knew she wouldn't get away without adding something to it. "I'll have a little chicken."

Instead, Dennis placed a good-size chicken breast on her plate and added a bit of seasoned brown rice.

"That's about the right amount for you, I think." He motioned to an empty section of the buffet. "I just put away the fruit platter. Give me a second." He scurried into the kitchen and came back with the large platter. "It's been picked over, but there are still lots of berries, if you'd like."

Hannah took a small serving bowl and pulled out blueberries, raspberries, strawberries and some blackberries. Then, with a big smile of thanks for Dennis, she grabbed a knife and fork and headed to a table out in the sunshine. She hadn't sat down for more than a few minutes when Sandra walked to her table.

"May I sit with you?"

Surprised and pleased, Hannah nodded. "Of course."

Sandra sat in the opposite chair. "You know? We've worked together for the last year, but it seems like because we work together, we never get the time to socialize."

"Isn't that the truth?" Hannah took a big bite of her Greek salad and smiled while she chewed. After the swallowed, she pointed at her plate. "Dennis fixed this for me. I do so love the food here."

Sandra nodded. "And Dennis always makes those of us here as happy as we can be."

"True enough." It took Hannah a few minutes to realize Sandra sat almost uncomfortably, as if waiting for something. Hannah glanced around. "Is something wrong?"

Sandra slumped a little bit in her chair. "I wanted to ask you something, as you seem to be the closest with Denton." She hesitated. "Has he said anything about why he might be upset with Cole?"

Hannah's eyebrows shot up, and she vigorously shook her head. "Oh, my goodness, no. I don't think there's anything wrong." And then she realized what he was trying to do and the rebound effect. She slowly lowered her fork to her tray. "There was something, but it wasn't Cole himself. It was more …" And she stopped. She didn't know if she should say anything. This was Denton's issue. Lamely she added, "It's not my place to discuss it, but I know he was being a little more independent and not quite so dependent on his friends."

Sandra studied her face. "You think that's all there is to it?"

Hannah nodded gently. "Absolutely."

Relief washed over Sandra's face. "That would be good to know. It felt a little bit like he'd been cut off. This isn't a place to be cut off from your friends."

"That's so very true. And I certainly don't think Denton wants Cole to feel in any way that he wasn't still his best friend or at least one of his two best friends." She'd have to mention to Denton how his silence and his goal for more independence had affected the others. And if Cole was feeling the change, Brock likely was too.

"Thanks for that, Hannah. I'll let you enjoy the rest of your food."

Hannah watched as Sandra got up and walked away. She'd been friendly. She wasn't sure that counted in her quest for friendship as she hadn't initiated the contact, but it was still nice.

She finished off her lunch, her thoughts swirling around closely entwined old friendships and how the different dynamics worked. After she returned her dirty dishes, she detoured to Denton's room. She knocked, but there was no answer. Feeling torn between happiness and concern, she headed to her office.

WHEN A KNOCK came at the door, it opened before Denton could greet his visitor, and he raised his head and frowned. Then his gaze lit up as Brock walked in.

He waited at the doorway for a moment, then nodded. "That's why I didn't wait for an answer," Brock said. "You've never been able to hide your feelings on your face, so I wanted to see if you have an issue with us or are genuinely glad to see us. No one knows what the hell is going on."

Denton winced. "Brock, I will always be glad to see you guys."

"Really? So how come you've been putting us off for days now? We usually meet for coffee or a meal, but lately, when we've stopped by, the door's often locked. You aren't initiating any contact." He walked in, pulled up a chair, turned it backward and sat down. "So what gives?"

Denton stared at him, feeling speechless.

"This sure as hell better not be the two of you having an issue with me," Cole declared from the doorway. "We've always been able to talk. We've always been able to deal with our issues, so what the hell is going on?"

Brock motioned for Cole to come in. "He was fine when I entered, a welcoming expression on his face, so I'll take that as a good sign."

Cole grabbed a second chair and sat. "Then why the hell have you been avoiding us?"

"Not so." The guys staring at him made Denton feel

bad. "I wasn't avoiding you."

"Okay, so what gives?"

He opened his mouth and then closed it, not sure how to start.

Brock jumped in. "Is it Hannah? You don't want to say anything to us because you found a girl?"

"Hell no. That's not the way we roll, and you know that." Denton hated to think his friends would blame Hannah. Like she didn't have enough problems making friends on her own already.

Cole nodded. "We've never had a problem before. But something is definitely going on, and one of the big changes that we see is that you and Hannah appear to be spending a lot of time together and getting pretty close."

"I sure hope we are," he blurted out, then stopped. "And wow, I didn't expect that answer."

"This is a good surprise?" Cole asked. "Because we've all been blindsided by the women who work here. It's not that we expect you to be any different. That means we've seen the signs that you couldn't see yet. We didn't see them at the beginning either. Not until our respective women had gotten in trouble or had issues, one way or another." Cole laughed. "You should be thanking us. Especially Brock, as he's been paving the way for the rest of us."

"Our leader once again," Denton said teasingly. But he had a big grin on his face, and his heart was warm and feeling so damn fine. "Okay, so the funny thing is, she and I talked about the fact that she's never had real friends. And how envious she was that we have the kind of friendship we have. It got me to thinking. What I liked about Hannah was the fact that she wasn't dependent on anyone. She stood strong even though she was alone, and it never seemed to bother her. Now I realize, of course, it bothers her, and I also realize she's had to do things in some ways to stand on her own to feel a little more secure."

The men sat back and stared at him.

"That's garbage," Cole said. "I'm sorry for Hannah if she doesn't have friends or hasn't experienced what it's like to be in something like our group, but to consider that she was better off alone or maybe had learned certain things you hadn't …" He shook his head. "Well, I don't see that."

Brock tilted his head and studied Denton. "There's more to it than that. Does it go back to your perception of yourself as a charity case for most of your life, and you're still afraid you are?"

"Dammit, Brock." Irritation flared in Denton's gut. "I got over that a long time ago."

Brock raised one eyebrow. "Did you?"

"Of course I did." He waved his arms wide. "I'm here. I'm delighted to be here. I'm not paying a penny for this. Somebody else is forking over that money. That's not my issue."

"Tell us—like it or not—how this could be deemed a charity case, how you feel like you never pulled your own weight because you've had so much help. And now you're afraid you won't stand on your own two feet because you have us?" Cole asked shrewdly.

Denton sat back and groaned. "It's not even like that so much. I noticed Hannah had an air of independence about her. Because she hasn't had friends and family around her. She's done everything herself. I'm not sure I would've made it through without you guys."

"So you're afraid that you can't do what she's doing? You can't do it on your own because you have friends?"

Denton felt pinned in place, like a bug under a magnifying glass. "I guess. I know it's kind of twisted around and upside down. Could you guys not make a big deal out of this? I wanted to see how I would do if I wasn't texting a dozen times in a day or seeing you guys every day."

Silence fell over the room.

Brock stared at him. "And so? What was the result?"

Cole gave Denton a lopsided grin, encouraging him to share with them.

"I understood a little bit about what she's going through," Denton said. "That loneliness that she's always had in her life. I didn't have the same experience she did, since I do know what it's like to have good friends. Friends who barge in my door to make sure I'm not hiding from them. Friends who understand how important our relationship is."

"So how does she feel about what you're doing?" Brock asked.

This time Denton chuckled. "Well, it's part of the challenge for me to separate slightly this last week and for her to step forward. To see if she could make some friends and be a little friendlier every day."

"I never noticed her not being friendly," Brock said with a frown.

"Exactly. But if you didn't see her with me, would you see her at all?"

The two men looked at him and then chuckled.

"Maybe not," Cole answered. "But then we are both seeing just one woman. And maybe that's why you see her. Because she's for you."

"No idea yet if she is or not. But I'd like to find out. However, I don't want to collect another friend because they need that relationship, and I don't want to be collected because she needs a relationship."

"Now we come to the crux of it all," Brock mused. "I think that's a very valid point. Enough so we can understand you figuring out this whole relationship thing. We're on board. I promise you."

"All the power to you," Cole added. "None of this relationship thing is easy. We've seen that she's sincere, honest and real. And you know how we feel about those qualities."

"Absolutely," Denton said. "And maybe that's why we had this initial attraction. Because she is all that. The sense that I can trust her. That she'd be there for me. And if she can accept what she sees now, then it can only get better, and yet, if I relapse, she'd take it in stride."

"So, it is that serious?" Cole grinned.

Denton shrugged and smiled too. "I'd like to think so, but I also think we have to wait and see."

Brock chuckled. "I feel like we should bring other single buddies of ours here. There is something magical about Hathaway House."

Cole laughed. "Don't tell Dani that. If she thought we were using this place as a matchmaking service, she'd run for the hills."

Denton shook his head. "Are you sure about that? From what I understand, she's the one who blazed this trail. I've heard Aaron always was a bit of a trailblazer. I'm sorry he's not here right now. I'd love to get to know him."

The men exchanged grins.

"Aaron is at school right now. According to Dani," Brock said, "he just finished a set of tough exams. He should be home soon."

"Good. Let's meet up with him when he's back."

Chapter 10

HANNAH CONTINUED TO go out of her way for the next few days to be friendly to everyone, even though she knew this general approach defeated her purpose to be a little more social and to do something for someone specific every day. If she did end up doing things with Denton, then it was a sure thing she would be doing things with the men around him. And that meant their women as well. That Hannah might become a part of their group, with her becoming the sixth member, had her feeling fuzzy inside.

Maybe the whole thing wasn't as much of an issue as she'd thought. It had taken a few days, but she'd noticed a shift. Everybody seemed friendlier toward her. It wasn't so much that she was making friends but that she was more open and welcoming and was getting the same kind of response back. Even the kitchen staff had noticed.

"Something must be good in your life right now," Dennis had said with a laugh, teasing her. "I've never seen you with so many smiles on your face."

"Really?" She winced. "Was I that unfriendly?" She trusted him to give her a truthful answer since Dennis was a straight shooter.

He shook his head. "Nope, not unfriendly, just not overly friendly. You've always had an air of reservation about you, as if you weren't quite sure if you were welcome."

That startled a laugh out of her. "That's exactly how I felt. I never attracted friends before, and I was always worried about my welcome. This is kind of an experiment," she admitted. "To see if I can work on making some friends. So I have to be friendlier."

"I wouldn't worry about that," he said with a shrug. "You're good people, and good people always find friends."

"I've never felt like I was *good people*."

"Listen," Dennis said, his expression serious. "Sometimes you choose the wrong group, or sometimes it's hard to meet people. When you've been hurt, it sometimes seems impossible. It's hard not to keep looking at everyone in the same negative way."

She stared at him in wonder. "And here I thought you worked in the kitchen. I didn't know you were a shrink. You've got real talent there."

That big grin of his flashed. He waved his cup of coffee, motioning to a fresh pot brewing right beside them. "It's just a matter of standing behind the counter, watching people day in and day out and understanding how much our existence here is simply a small view of the real world out there. People grow. People change, and sometimes you can't see who they are. As a staff member, I see how people treat me. In a supposedly lower-paying job like this one," he said, "you see people's true colors. But for the most part, those who are here have been very good to me."

"Good. I'd hate to think you were being slighted in any way. You've always got a smile for everyone, and you're one of the most helpful people on staff. I would be lost without you."

He chuckled as he gave the counter a wipe. "And that's very kind of you to say. The thing is, I don't think you see yourself as you really are. I've never seen you *ever* have a sour word for anyone. You always have a smile on your face, and you're always here ready to do the job, regardless of the night you had or how someone spoke to you. It's not an easy job. None of this is. But there are rewards"—he shook his head—"and those rewards are tremendous. It's not about the money in your bank account. It's about your day-to-day experiences and that little bit of yourself offered to everyone else. Don't try so hard to make friends or to be friendly. Just be yourself."

"That'd be terrific, but I haven't made many friends so far," she pointed out to him.

"Because you weren't open to it. That's one of the biggest things—you will make friends if you are open to the concept. That is a matter of how many people walk in front of you. Do you see them or not?" He gave her a small wave with his towel and headed back into the kitchen.

Hannah wasn't sure what happened, but it felt like she'd gotten a lecture on life.

"Wow," a man behind her murmured.

She spun in surprise to see Shane behind her. "Right? Who knew Dennis was so deep?"

Shane shook his head. "I didn't know, and I've been working with him for six years."

"He is very good at what he does, and obviously he understands people in a way we don't." She frowned slightly. "You know? It'd be very good for every one of us to stand on the other side of that counter for a few days and watch the world walk past—the good, the bad and the ugly."

"Do I have to?" Shane asked. "I wouldn't want my hands so near the food. I'd gain forty pounds in a month."

She burst into laughter. "You? Overweight? That would

be something to see."

He gave her a mock look of horror. "Bite your tongue. I work hard to keep all that lovely food prepared here for us off my waistline."

"So far, I haven't had to do too much work in that area. I do eat, but I have a high metabolism."

"True, but one day your metabolism will slow down. And you will pay the price."

It was her turn to look at him. "Now *you* bite *your* tongue," she snapped laughingly. "I wouldn't know what to do in a gym. I've never felt comfortable in those places."

"Never say never," Shane said. "Many of us workout here. You are more than welcome to join us anytime."

She shook her head. "Oh, no thank you. That would be incredibly awkward for me."

He stopped, studying her for a moment. "I guess if you've never been in there, it's intimidating."

"Very intimidating. I wouldn't know what to do or where to start. I'd be afraid of hurting myself on the first day."

He nodded. "Let's do something about that. Normally I do a forty-minute workout at the end of the day. Why not meet me? We can go through something very basic, very simple, that you can do on your own without any awkwardness."

She wanted to refuse. But then her brain poked at her. It was one of the few invitations she'd ever received at Hathaway. She wrinkled her nose up at him. "Is getting sweaty a requirement?"

He burst into laughter. "It's a definite requirement."

She sighed. "Okay. I'll try it once, and if it's too …" She was at a loss for words.

"Too what? Too heavy? Too painful? Or too sweaty to return to work?"

At her nod, he wrapped an arm around her shoulders. "The gym can be adapted for whatever you need and whatever you feel comfortable with. Nothing is written in stone. Just pick a day and join me." He poured himself a cup of coffee and took a bite of his cinnamon bun. "I work out so I can have these. That's the only reason why."

"Because you love food."

His eyes lit up. "Exactly." He grinned at her and gave her a wink before disappearing down the hallway.

Well, now she'd done it. She'd gotten herself signed up for a workout with Shane. Suddenly, she was afraid the whole thing would be a huge disappointment, and she'd make a fool of herself.

But at least he had offered. Which was a success.

Suddenly feeling happier at the concept, she returned to the coffee pot. She refilled her mug and after a moment, poured a cup for Dani too. As she placed the mugs on a tray, she glanced at the fresh hot cinnamon buns and decided she and Dani both needed the treat. She grabbed the laden tray and headed to Dani's office.

As she walked toward the main office, she caught sight of a horse trailer pulling down the driveway. She paused outside Dani's office and watched as the trailer made its way to the far end of the building. She glanced at Dani. "You've got more horses coming?"

Dani lifted her head from her desk and looked at her in confusion. "Horses? I don't think so. Why?"

Hannah put the tray down on her desk. "Well, a horse trailer pulled up the drive and headed toward Stan's end of the building."

Dani hopped up and walked to the front door to take a look. "As soon as I've had coffee and that treat—thank you, by the way," she said, "I'll head down there to see what that's all about."

"Do you mind if I come with you?" Hannah offered. "I've seen the horses here but only from afar."

"You're kidding, right?" Dani's expression was one of disbelief.

Hannah chuckled. "Nope. I never had the opportunity to ride a horse before. I haven't been around a real horse."

After finishing their coffee and pastries, Dani headed down the hallway. "That'll change right now. Come with me."

DENTON ROSE, FINISHING the last set of calf raises, his muscles shaking with the effort. The workout today had been hard and demanding, and he was so done.

"That was a great effort," Shane said approvingly. "You pushed that movement to the max. Don't forget to have your snack as soon as you get back to your room."

Denton laughed wryly. "It seems nobody lets me forget about my little lapse."

Shane shook his head. "Hell no. Not in a place like this. Dennis won't blab about it, but he's certainly on top of things too. And if it looks like you're suffering or struggling in any way, he will mention it to one of us on your team."

"Considering it's all done in my best interests, it's a little hard to get upset about it."

"That's the spirit."

"How is it that even missing a toe is such a major injury?

How can it have such a brutal effect on my body?"

"It's pretty amazing how much something like that affects everything else."

Denton's hamstrings were killing him as he did one more muscle exercise. "Another question—how can muscles that are no longer there hurt?"

"Are you hurting badly today?" Shane gave him a crooked grin and said, "If not, pick it up."

At that, Denton laughed out loud. "I guess you've heard all the excuses and procrastination delays anybody can give."

Shane nodded his head. "When you work at a place like this, you don't run short on those. Remember to dig in to work on the slow, controlled movement. For that burn that says something is happening. You're building muscles, which means you must make tiny micro tears into the existing muscle, so it can rebuild bigger and stronger. If the muscles are new, they must be fired awake again. Nerve endings can be painful. You know perfectly well how this works. When it all comes together, it's a piece of art."

"I'm a work in progress." Denton closed his eyes, feeling the pain shoot up his legs, the back of his ankle, even his knees. Missing a hamstring muscle made it harder. But it wasn't bad. It could be so much worse. At least he had his legs. From what he'd seen here, a lot of guys were way worse off. When he finally finished his set, his body was completely drenched in sweat.

"There you go," Shane said. "Nice job."

"Am I supposed to be so worked up over this?"

"Absolutely. It's like hitting a wall. You feel like it's taken everything out of you right now. When you rebuild, you come back stronger and bigger and better than ever."

Denton nodded. "Good to know."

They went to work on other muscles, focusing on balancing both sides of his body. By the time his session with Shane was done, Denton was drenched. He shook his head. "I'm hitting the showers."

Shane nodded. "Or you can go to the pool."

Denton lit up like a firecracker. "Really? I thought it would be longer before I hit the pool."

"You've been cleared, so how about today? You worked hard. Your body could do with the cooldown."

"Sounds even better," Denton said. "I'll get my swim trunks and meet you down there."

"I'll be with you for about twenty minutes, and then I have another physiotherapy session in the pool. So I can't keep an eye on you while I work with the other person. That okay?"

Denton knew what Shane was asking. "Yes, I'm perfectly capable of going in the water on my own. I'm ecstatic to have a chance to hit that hot tub. And thank you for the confidence in my ability and independence."

With a high-five, they separated. Denton had a new surge of energy at the thought of the pool and the hot tub, and he made his way quickly to his room. His shirt clung to his back as sweat dripped from his scalp. But knowing where he was going made all the difference. Deciding the wheelchair might be more prudent, he sat down and wheeled his way to the elevator, his towel wrapped around his shoulders. He slowly made his way to the pool deck and wondered what the protocol was.

Shane appeared at his side. "First things first. Because you came from a workout, you need a quick shower before you get into the pool. Afterward you can get right in the water."

Denton realized Shane was already in his own bathing trunks. Fit and lean, he was a great role model. Denton was seriously excited. Containing his exuberance, he made his way to the changing room and parked the wheelchair outside. Denton rinsed off and then made his way very slowly to the pool's edge, surveying all the amenities disabled people might need, including a motorized lift for getting in and out. "No money spared here, huh?"

"No, when it came to putting in the pool, Dani and the Major did it right."

"And we all get the benefit of that." He stood for a moment, struck with hesitation. What was the easiest way for him to get in?

"Don't worry about it. Just jump in," Shane said, chuckling.

Denton flashed him a big grin and fell sideways into the water. Cool waves wrapped around his body. He'd always been a water baby, and he couldn't believe how much he'd missed it. As he slowly sank, his body instantly reacted, bending and swerving, kicking and waving, the motion so damn natural it almost brought tears to his eyes. When he broke the surface, he closed his eyes for a long moment, enjoying the sensation of once again being back in his natural environment.

"Glad to see I don't need to worry about you in the water," Shane said jokingly.

"I *was* a Navy SEAL," he said with a grin. For him that said it all. He closed his eyes and floated in joy.

Life could be a lot worse.

Chapter 11

ONCE AGAIN, HANNAH marveled at the joys of her job. How many people got to spend an hour visiting with horses in the middle of their workday? She met Maggie and Molly, the baby, who stood in attendance. Hannah watched as a new arrival was unloaded.

"This is Sir Raleigh," Stan said. "He's a racehorse. Destined for the factory."

Dani's face turned grim. "And will he fit in with the other horses?"

Stan chuckled. "The last time we talked, you told me to rescue any horse I knew of. He's still intact. I figured we could give him a quick surgical procedure and put him out to pasture along with the others."

Dani's face broke into a beautiful smile. "So very glad to hear that. I was a little concerned about the stallion aspect, but if we can castrate him, then that's fine."

"Should've been done a long time ago, after his stallion days were well and truly gone. He's very old, so in that aspect, they wouldn't bother with the surgery. Yet, it would've made him a lot easier to handle. I'm equipped here to perform the surgery, so I will take care of that in the next couple of days, and then he'll be fine to be pastured with the mares, particularly given his age."

Stan was right. Hannah watched the two men maneuvering Sir Raleigh into a stall. He blew and stomped slightly in outrage but more for show. He wasn't rearing back, and he wasn't kicking anybody, so he had been well trained. "He doesn't appear to be adjusting too badly."

"He might already have a good idea what's happening too," Dani replied.

Hannah winced, thinking about the glue factory. "I'm sure he'll have a lovely life here."

Once Sir Raleigh had settled, Stan stepped in and did a quick exam. The horse stood quiet. But by the way he stood, Hannah could see he was proud. Every inch a stallion.

"I'm surprised they would get rid of him."

"The stallion is only good for one thing," Dani murmured. "And if his offspring aren't showing the promise they had hoped for, then it's not worth even that."

"It's a tough life."

Dani stepped inside the stall and held out her hand. Hannah watched from the safety of the gate. The stallion smelled Dani and then blew gently on her hand. She stroked his long nose. "You'll be just fine here, boy. We'll make sure you get another ten to fifteen years of good living."

Hannah watched in amazement as the horse calmed down under the tender care of Stan and Dani. Within minutes, Sir Raleigh was led to fresh hay and water. He started to eat and drink. "When will you let him out to feed on the green grass?" Dani asked.

"It'll be much easier to deal with him confined here," Stan answered. "After the procedure, we will give him a day out in the pasture on his own, and then we'll slowly introduce him to the mares."

"There are only females in the pasture. Right?"

"That's correct. I have only one gelding, the others are

mares. But once he's gelded and calmed down slightly, he'll blend in."

"Gelded?" Hannah asked.

Dani chuckled. "Stallions tend to maintain their personalities, even after being gelded. He will remain somewhat aggressive and hard to handle, and he will still think the mares are his."

"So, a male is a male?" Hannah asked.

Stan shot her a mock look while Dani chuckled. "Exactly."

"Dani, you have built something special here. I can't imagine where these animals would've ended up without your help," Hannah said.

"Not just the animals. Think of all the injured people upstairs." Stan shook his head. "Even staff members who don't work out so well in other places do better here."

Hannah laughed. "Dani collects cast-off animals, injured patients and cranky staff."

"I don't collect anything," Dani protested. "I'm just trying to help."

"And a fine job she does too," Denton said.

Hannah turned to see Denton in his wheelchair. His hair was wet, and although he looked tired, he also had a very happy smile on his face.

"Don't you look like you've had a great day," she said in a teasing voice.

"Oh, I did, indeed. I got in the pool for the first time today."

"Now that makes sense. I don't use it enough," Hannah said.

"No time like the present," Denton said. "Although, if you want company in the water, it won't be me. I'm tired today. About to go up and change and head for dinner."

The group slowly broke up as everyone returned to the main building. Hannah took the opportunity to walk with Denton to the elevator and upstairs.

"I'll be a little bit. I still have some work to do in the office," she confessed. "Dani had a new horse arrive, so I came down with her to see him."

"Are you a horse-crazy girl too?"

"No." She shook her head with a startled laugh. "I haven't been around them at all. I find them fairly intimidating," she confessed.

"I get that. They're large animals. Lots of people here look after them. But I know some of the staff and the patients go down and visit with them all the time."

"I get down to Stan's stomping grounds to bring certain animals to integrate with the patients. Chickie and Helga are two of my favorites. But it's part of my job, so I don't get to linger down there."

"And I haven't spent much time with them at all."

"Stop by the office. When I left, Chickie was sleeping on his bed."

"Sure. I can stop by there first."

Together they walked into her office, and sure enough, Chickie was curled up in a ball. As soon as they walked in, he lifted his head and gave a small yelp. She picked him up, and he snuggled close. She glanced over at Denton.

"I'm soaking wet," he said wryly. "I need to rinse off and change, and in the meantime, it looks like Chickie could use some loving." His smile flashed. "Give me twenty minutes, and I'll be back. Maybe he'll sit with me."

Hannah sat in her chair and carefully tucked Chickie into her lap and quickly went through the rest of her work for the afternoon. In the back of her mind she wondered if maybe she'd get an invitation to have dinner with Denton too. If nothing else, for coffee before.

She gently stroked Chickie's head. "You're a lucky thing. You get to visit with him." When she heard slow footsteps approaching, she looked up to see Denton arriving at the doorway. She smiled. "No wheelchair?"

"That was the easy way. I was thinking that maybe, if I could walk to dinner and then make the trip back again, I could rest in my room for the remainder of the evening. I hate to take the easy route, but at the same time, I worry about overdoing it."

"And without the wheelchair, do you want to hold Chickie?"

He flashed her a grin and gave her a bashful look. "I was kind of hoping you'd be done for the day and could have coffee with me."

She laughed out loud and hopped to her feet, holding Chickie gently in her arms. "And here I was hoping to have dinner with you."

The two stared at each other, feeling that instant rapport.

"Then how about we do both, and you can tell me how you're getting on." He glanced around the room. "Are you done here?"

She nodded and shut down the computer. With Chickie in her arms, the two of them walked to the dining hall.

"Inside or out?"

"Outside right now. We can always find a seat closer to the food when it's ready."

"You sound like you're hungry," she teased.

"That I am."

117

DALE MAYER

When they found seats in the sun, he sat down, and she delivered Chickie to him before walking to the coffee bar. She picked up a tray with two cups filled with black coffee and returned to the table.

"I couldn't remember if you take creamer in your coffee or sugar or both."

"Cream is good, thanks."

Chickie looked up and sniffed the air as Hannah placed the creamer tubs and sugar packets on the table.

"It must be hard not to have everybody feed him," Denton said, scratching the pup behind his ears.

She nodded. "Especially with Chickie. His system is very touchy. If he has anything other than his dietary food, it causes him a great deal of pain."

She watched as Denton gently stroked Chickie's small tan-colored body. Chickie shifted slightly to sit deeper in Denton's lap and closed his eyes.

"Unlike a lot of dogs," she said, "he spends a lot of time sleeping."

"Maybe that's best for him at this stage." He lifted his gaze and looked at her. "So, give me an update on how your friend thing is working out."

She winced. "Maybe good? Maybe I'm doing it for all the wrong motives, and that's not so good." She shrugged, not wanting to share how wrong her motives could be related to him. He was quickly becoming someone she wanted to be so much more than a friend with, and yet she didn't know what he wanted. What if he just wanted to be friends? How did that work? For her it wouldn't work at all. "I want to be a little more relaxed about it."

"Everything is negotiable. And you're right. You can't force it to work either." He studied her for a long moment.

"So ... is there anybody who you decided to befriend?"

She winced. "Well, there is somebody I'd like to be a little friendlier with, but I don't know how that will work out."

He sent a sharp glance her way. "Friendlier? Or like really friendly?"

She flushed. "It's kind of personal."

"Personal's what friends do," he said. "But I didn't realize you were sweet on anybody here."

"I didn't realize it either." She stared at her coffee cup and wrinkled her nose. "But that's the thing about opening yourself up, looking at other people as friends. It tends to open you up to other feelings at the same time."

An awkward silence followed. She raised her gaze to look at him, wondering how he took her news. She had been deliberately vague about it.

He continued to study her intently.

She could feel her flush deepen and darkened. She raised an eyebrow. "What?"

He leaned forward. "Who?"

HE WATCHED AS she settled back in her chair, shaking her head.

"Not sure I'm ready to say anything about it yet," she confessed. She dropped her gaze instead of staring at him directly.

Why was he pushing her again? He'd been hoping he was the one she was sweet on. If she wouldn't say anything, how the hell was he supposed to know? That was what he liked about his buds. They were all direct—they spoke up when they had something to say. And Denton never had to finesse anything nor figure out the rules of dating. But it had seemed to him that he and Hannah were working toward something that wasn't just friendship.

"Do you consider me your friend?" she asked.

He raised an eyebrow and nodded. "Certainly, the beginning of a friendship anyway."

"Not in the same vein as Brock and Cole of course," she added. "I wondered how that worked."

He settled in his seat, holding on to Chickie as he shifted. "We were already working on being friends. I want you to find somebody else to do something nice for every day."

"No, I am," she rushed to reassure him. "Every day I'm spending more time around people. I spent quite a bit of time with Stan and Dani today. Which was nice and unusual at the same time. But it was fun."

He relaxed slightly. "Is it Shane?" He hadn't meant to come right out and ask who she was sweet on, but it was disturbing and would eat at Denton until he knew for sure. He had hoped that something was between them, not that she was looking for someone else. He wondered if he should encourage her to choose him for her acts of kindness. At least then he'd know she cared. He hadn't made any claims or presumed to be so forward as to throw his hat into the ring, so she had no idea of his feelings.

"*Is it Shane* what?"

"The guy you're sweet on?"

"Oh, my goodness, no." She leaned forward and grasped Denton's hands. "Not at all. Shane's a sweetheart. But we're friends. And I like that."

Relief settled inside him. Still Denton frowned. "Now you have me thinking about every male in the place, wondering who it is."

She gave him an odd look, then picked up her coffee cup and took a drink. "Maybe it isn't anything anyway. Just a passing fancy. How does one even begin to know?"

He couldn't stop thinking about who the person could be. "Whenever they come into the room, it's like the room lightens and brightens and becomes so much warmer and cozier. You look up to see if they are walking into the room, even though you know there's absolutely no way they could be here because they are away. But you can't help yourself, hoping they'll be here." He gave her a crooked grin. "They're the last thing on your mind when you go to sleep, and they're the first thing on your mind when you wake up because they've been in your dreams all night with you."

Her mouth opened ever-so-slightly, her eyes going wide. "Oh my, that sounds wonderful."

"It is," he said, unsettled. Because only one person was always on his mind. And it was her. He watched Hannah, wondering what the hell just happened to his world. And how cruel could the world be if that was how he felt, and she had chosen somebody else.

Then Brock and Cole walked in. Denton waved at them, relieved to see this distraction from his tortuous thoughts.

She took a cue from that and stood.

"You're not staying for dinner?" he asked. He was disappointed to see her leave, particularly when she had said she'd hoped to have dinner with him. "I thought maybe you wanted to talk about something."

She cast a sideways glance at the men approaching. "Another time." And she walked to the rack of dirty dishes and placed her cup with them, then came and took Chickie from him.

He watched as she made her escape from the dining room. He frowned. His buddies plunked down on chairs beside him.

"We didn't mean to chase her away. Sorry for intruding on your private moment."

He glanced at Brock. "I'm not sure what you intruded on."

"What do you mean by that?" Cole asked.

Denton explained the odd conversation they'd had as he gazed from one friend to the other. "But she left. We were supposed to have dinner together, but you guys showed up, and she walked out." He shrugged. "Not sure what to make of any of it." First came silence at the table, and then Brock and Cole chuckled.

Denton frowned at them both. "What's up?"

"The mysterious person she's sweet on is you. And when you didn't pick up on her cues, she didn't know quite what to make of it."

He stared at them and frowned. "What? What was I supposed to say? I asked if she was sweet on Shane."

At that Cole laughed. "Everybody here loves Shane, but I don't think he has anybody special."

"But maybe that's who she has feelings for," Denton argued. Inside, he wondered if they were right. He tried to think back on the odd conversation as if he'd missed something, and maybe a second pass would show him what it was. "I'd like for you guys to be right, but I don't see it."

"We'll find out from our ladies if Hannah's been spending time with anyone," Cole said. "But I don't believe it's anyone else but you. You have to give her the right cues and let her know where she stands, that's all."

"Okay." But he wondered, "If that's what she meant,

then I've screwed up. Because I didn't give her any kind of response to that."

"Do you want to?"

Denton looked down at his broken body still on the mend. "It's hardly the best timing."

"I understand why you say that," Brock said slowly, "but I think you're wrong. I think if ever we needed to show up as the people we truly are, then today is the day for it." Brock shrugged. "If there's one thing I've learned in my new relationship, it's how she wants honesty on all levels. I'm no longer the big warrior I was. I'm no longer a SEAL. But what I am is a lot more realistic for her. I'm a lot more me. My integrity is intact. My ethics, my moral code all are intact, and I'm still the warrior even today. Just another variety."

Cole nodded. "That's so very true. We aren't the people we once were. But who we are now is authentic. Don't try to be anything else, and don't wait to be any better. Don't wait till your body heals and you're as good as you can be. Because there can always be setbacks. You'll live life now with a whole different set of health issues. We can be stronger, more vibrant, able to take on the world, but that doesn't mean when we have an issue or get set back, that we don't want somebody who'll be there for us, knowing what we were like before. You don't want to go into a relationship looking for perfection or expecting it. It doesn't exist. You can't have it, and the last thing you want to do is to present yourself in that light. The reality is, this is who you are."

Denton stared at the table. "So how do I fix this?"

The other two men shared a glance, then shrugged. "That's up to you," Brock said. "You'll find a way. And on that note, are we eating dinner together?"

Denton nodded. "I got stood up, so I guess so."

Cole patted him on the shoulder. "The food's ready, so come on. Let's get in line before everyone else joins in."

Denton nodded, and with the others ahead of him, he slowly made his way to the buffet. But inside his head, he kept remembering how she had said she was hoping to have dinner with him. When his buddies came, something had changed. He had figured that, maybe afterward, he and Hannah could go for an evening swim and have coffee and dessert. He stood in the line with the guys and pulled out his phone to send her a text.

I wish you had stayed, but I'm eating dinner with the guys. Meet me for coffee and dessert at the pool later?

He held his phone tightly in his hand as he studied the food, waiting for her answer. Finally, when it came, she'd included a happy face.

Sure. One hour?

A grin whispered across his face. **Yes**, he typed. **That would be perfect.**

Brock edged toward him. "By that expression on your face, I'm guessing your love life is better?"

Denton nodded. "If it's my love life, then it's better. But if she's after somebody else ..." He shook his head. "It might be time to find out for certain."

"So where will the romantic evening be?"

"I'll tell you, but make sure you guys are going in the opposite direction," he said. "We're meeting by the pool for coffee and dessert."

Brock rolled his eyes. "That pool has a lot to answer for."

The men chuckled. Denton followed slowly as they walked along the buffet, collecting everything they could possibly want to eat—a huge delicious-looking baked ham, brown rice, and lots of vegetables. Denton was tired, and he remembered Shane's suggestion to eat a lot of protein. With a slice of hot ham on his plate and a couple scoops of sides, Denton grabbed his cutlery and slowly made his way to the table. He would enjoy his dinner.

But he would enjoy the rest of his evening more.

Chapter 12

HANNAH DECIDED SHE'D go for a swim before meeting Denton. She'd done a lot of thinking about her life since his arrival. Figuring out what it was that had changed so much. Because something had indeed changed—she just wasn't exactly sure what. She'd met literally dozens of people here in the last year—patients, staff, support workers, family members—and then all the delivery vehicle drivers, etc. And in all that time, none of them had influenced her the way Denton did. Partly because she could see their friendship blossom. Partly because she had noticed some friendships were debilitating. As somebody who had spent so much time thinking about friends, that wasn't an easy thing to watch—it made her feel terrible.

She could never have explained why she worried about it. She had mentioned it earlier to Denton but hadn't gone into detail. It wasn't her place, but as soon as the opportunity presented itself, she would consider telling him. There was nothing wrong in finding security in numbers.

All she wanted was to have more friends. She finally realized that having friends was an important part of life.

Friendships were also important for their own healing abilities. Life was such a surprising mix of people; she couldn't help but wonder if she hadn't screwed up somewhere along the line. Screwed up in a way she had no right to.

She didn't want to be the girlfriend who split up her boyfriend's long-term group of male friends.

She wasn't a psychiatrist, a medical doctor, a therapist, or counselor. Maybe her comment to Denton about distancing himself from his friends was taking Denton too far from Brock and Cole. She didn't want that. Not in any way. She owed Denton an apology. As she slowly swam from one end of the pool to the other, taking her time, diving and floating, her mind kept running over the issues, feeling the pain and the regret. And the worry. Why hadn't she considered this evolution earlier?

There was more to work on, but she hadn't given it much thought. It hadn't hit her until she saw his two friends walking toward him and realized the distance Denton had put between the three of them was wrong because Brock and Cole didn't do anything wrong. She had. She now realized the impact her words had on people. The impact her being here had on people. She shouldn't have separated Brock and Cole from Denton. She shouldn't have had anything to do with that. She should've kept her mouth shut, and the fact that she hadn't was incredibly disturbing.

When she broke through the surface of the water, she had a newfound sense of resolve.

She knew what she needed to do, but it wouldn't be easy. And if it turned out badly, she could change her mind. That wouldn't be good because it could end up with her losing her job. But she'd rather lose her job than have Denton lose his friends. Because it wasn't just Denton who was affected but also Brock and Cole. And that was not good. She walked to the shallow end of the pool, her heart heavy.

"There you are." Denton stood nearby smiling down at her.

"Hi. Did you have a good dinner?"

He nodded. "It's always good to spend time with my friends."

She nodded, but inside she hurt. Because of course, he hadn't been spending time with his friends because of her. She grabbed her towel and slowly made her way out.

"Did you eat?" Denton asked.

"I had some salad. I wanted a swim first. I'll grab something more now." She dried off, grabbed her beach cover-up and threw it over her bathing suit. She didn't have any issues with her body, but she was extremely unhappy with who she was inside right now. And that sense of vulnerability hurt. She walked beside him. "You want to grab a table for coffee?"

He grinned and said cheerfully, "Dennis is bringing it over."

She chuckled. "Good. That saves me a trip, and Dennis is a sweetheart."

"I heard my name," Dennis called out from the stairs.

She glanced over to see him enter the pool area, a large tray in his hand. The evening sun was setting, and they chose a table off to the side, still bathed in the sun's glow.

Hannah sat in one of the chairs, still rubbing her hair with her towel. "This looks lovely."

"Well, I knew you were coming down here, and you didn't eat much earlier," Dennis said. "So this is a hot beef sandwich and a Greek salad—which I know you love—and coffee and desserts for you both. Enjoy." Then he turned and walked upstairs.

"Thank you," Hannah and Denton said together.

Denton chuckled. "Some of the people here seem so perfect for their roles. Like they really enjoy their lives and what they do for everyone."

"Isn't that the truth?" She stared at the roast beef sandwich and smiled. "And you know something? He's right. I am hungry." She dug into her sandwich and ate it without taking a break.

"You were hungry."

She grabbed a napkin, wiped her fingers and then her face and nodded. "I didn't think I was at first, but there's nothing quite like swimming and a little bit of worry to get somebody's appetite going."

"Not me. When I get worried, I can't eat."

"I'm the opposite," she said. "When I'm worried or upset, food becomes therapy."

"And yet, you are still slim."

She shrugged. "Metabolism. Apparently it's gonna catch up with me later." She gave him a smile. "But so far, I've been lucky."

"Besides, what can you possibly be worried about?"

She shook her head and stayed quiet, choosing to sip her coffee instead.

"Is it something that you can't share with a friend?" he teased.

"It's not that so much as I'm afraid I've done something wrong. I'm finally realizing the impact my words have on other people."

He slowly lowered his own cup of coffee. "Wow, that sounds serious."

She settled back into her chair. "It is. I just don't know how serious."

"Well, I'm here, available to listen, anytime you want to

talk."

She winced. Should she? Or should she talk it over with somebody else first? Had she done something to harm him? At the same time she didn't know if it had affected him at all. "Maybe I'm worrying for nothing."

"So tell me, and then I can help you."

She stared down at her coffee on the table. "It concerns you."

There, she had said it. She took a deep breath and let it out slowly, watching his reaction. He lowered his cup of coffee, his gaze darkening. She didn't know what was going on behind his gaze—she was afraid he'd get mad at her.

He leaned forward slightly in his chair. "Tell me."

She gave a small shrug. "I'm worrying that my comments about you being too dependent on your friends had a negative effect and gave you a bad reason to distance yourself from them."

He settled back into his chair and studied her for a long moment.

She felt the silence. She wasn't entirely comfortable with that, but until he spoke up, she couldn't do a lot. She wanted to rush in and fill the void with nonsense or make excuses, but something told her to hold her peace.

"And you're worried about that?"

She nodded.

"The thing is, you were correct. I was extremely dependent on my friends, and it never even occurred to me until you said that."

She winced. "But I didn't want to come between you and your friends."

He chuckled. "See? That's where your inexperience with how good friends work comes into play." He lifted his mug again. "Just because I needed some space and distance to figure out how much my neediness was affecting my own healing and my ability to move forward, it didn't affect their relationships with me."

"Yes, it did. Sandra came by and asked about you, wondering why you would distance yourself."

"Of course they were worried *for* me and *about* me. But they weren't worried I didn't care about them anymore. Their worry was that something was going on outside of me that they didn't know about, and they didn't know how to help. They were offering me support then they backed away and let me do my thing."

"Did they ask you what you were upset about?"

He nodded. "To some extent. The result was that they understood, but they thought I was being foolish."

"And are you?"

He shrugged. "Maybe. But I needed to examine it. I needed to look back on the situation from childhood to see if it was true or false. And for that, I thank you."

She stared at the table for a long moment, wondering if it really was that simple. She gave a sigh. "Thank you. I'm still not sure you understand the effect this could have on you and your friends. And I'm afraid that I may have caused a problem that isn't so easily resolved."

"You didn't cause a problem. You created an awareness of something I needed to look at. I decided I was extremely dependent, and I have spoken to my counselor and my shrink about it extensively in the last few days. And I know you're probably worried I'm upset and angry at you for pointing it out, but I'm delighted you did."

She sat back in surprise. "Well …"

He chuckled. "Right? And here you were, worried about

it all for nothing."

She shook her head. "I was thinking about all the people I've met since I arrived here last year and how a few of them have made an impact on me. I've seen inner strength in others who have surmounted incredible obstacles. Obstacles I've never been challenged to overcome. I found some incredible people who have done some incredible things. Their attitudes have been phenomenal. And it's made me look at who I am. Made me realize how lucky I am and how grateful I am to be here. To meet these wonderful people and learn about the reality of living an authentic life from them. I have a lot to learn," she admitted. "But the people I've met here have taught me more than I realized."

"Absolutely. That's one of the big things I have always said. When I woke up in the hospital and saw the extent of my injuries, I knew I got away lucky. I still had all four limbs. I still had a body that could stand upright. That was a powerful motivator to do some of things I had never had a chance to do before. And I felt truly blessed. There were days when I was dark and angry and hating life, wondering why this had happened to me in the first place. But there were so many good things about it I quickly moved on."

She nodded. "That's one of the things I like about you. Your ability to see the sunshine. Most people here don't get there for quite a while."

He leaned forward. "Don't forget. I recuperated in the hospital for a long while. I was late coming here compared to the others. Brock's injuries were much more severe than mine. His recuperation has been longer and harder. Yet, he did it in such a fine style I had to stand up and do my best to face my injuries with the same courage."

AS HE SAID the words, he could feel the truth of them rippling through him. Words he never expected to say. He'd never been one to analyze things like that. There were just so many things he could do without having to stop and spend time in deep thinking. And yet, he thought about all the benefits of having friends. Benefits he had depended on when he first got here. Emotions and needs he hadn't even discussed or contemplated before, and having nothing to do with him getting injured but from way back in his childhood. Okay, maybe his childhood issues influenced his initial emotions about his injuries. So, she had been right to bring it all up. In fact, he was glad she had because he'd had no way of seeing it without her comment.

He'd taken his relationships with Cole and Brock for granted.

And that wasn't good. What she wanted for him, and what he wanted for himself, was to know he could do this without his friends, a complete either/or situation. Either fully engaged with his friends or not engaged at all unless Brock or Cole reached out to Denton. To know that his healing would come about whether Cole and Brock were here or not. They were damn good people, and he was proud to call them friends. But he also knew he couldn't afford to let something happen to that friendship. Which, considering they both had partners, was possible.

"Denton, you seem awfully somber. Are the worries of the world sitting on your shoulders?"

He lifted his head, then shrugged. "No, not at all. I'm blessed to have friends in my life, but I need to know I can handle whatever comes my way, even if they're not here.

They are great people, and I'm honored, but time changes everything. Maybe that's why I was desperate to come here. Because, after my accident, I knew I'd do well here because they were here. We were all injured within months of each other, which seemed to be part of that same ongoing theme. But I also needed to know I could recover here without them."

"Well, that time is now, is it not? Isn't Brock moving on soon?"

Denton nodded. "He is. He's hoping to find a job working in Dallas. He still has to find a place to live, so I'll see him for a while, but he won't be here every day after that."

She nodded. "That sounds like progress. A necessary progress in a whole different way for him as well."

Denton smiled. "Absolutely. And once again he's leading the way. He always did in our relationships. With every group of friends you have different strengths, and Brock was always a good one for charging forward and letting us know what the weather would be like up ahead."

"I think that's a lovely thing," she said warmly. "And just because you're considering all this, it does not mean you aren't capable of doing everything you want to."

He sat back and chuckled. "It's interesting how you have minimal friends and have been alone most of your life while I come from a large SEAL family, a big support group, lots of friends. We each have something the other would like to have."

"I can't say too many people have said that to me before," she said. "Most of the time people see me as standoffish, reserved, maybe even cold."

"All of which are completely different and have no bearing on who you really are. They might think you're reserved, and you could be because you don't present yourself as super friendly. Hence what you're working on. And yet, at the same time, you're independent, and that can be threatening to people. As if you don't need anybody, and if you don't need them, a lot of times they are not sure what their role is in a relationship with you."

"That's a harsh way to look at relationships."

He shook his head. "Not at all. They are bringing something different than what you have to offer into a friendship. That's normal. We each offer something different. We each need something different. As you're making me see that I've needed that support. To know that somebody was there for me. To know I wasn't alone handling what I had to handle."

She winced.

He rushed to reassure her. "I'm not saying it's a bad thing. You are so capable of handling your problems alone. This is a good thing."

She laughed. "I'm not sure how it can be. But if you say so."

"It's a very good thing, if you think about it. Look at how much more you've learned about yourself. That's important. What I've learned about me doesn't change my friendship with Brock and Cole, and it doesn't change how much I need or want them in my life. It helps in a different way. It helps me grow as a person. Part of me came here feeling like I didn't belong. I wasn't as badly hurt as so many I see, including my friend Cole, who has a harder road to travel. But I'm here to help him. I was thinking that their presence helps me."

"And you've given me a great reminder that friendship is about giving and taking. And although I was saying the words, I wasn't following up with the actions."

Chapter 13

" **A** ND YOU ALSO have to remember," she said, "you are injured. Several times you said you aren't as badly injured as the others. There is no comparison here. You came because you needed help. You came because this was the place to get your physical body back as good as it could be, and along with that comes the work to make the mental and psychological aspects of yourself whole as well. It doesn't matter how you are when you arrive. You still deserve to be here. You still deserve to have your friends around you, pulling for you, rooting for you. It's almost like you've been overly friendly all this time because you feel guilty."

He tilted his head, frowned. "Guilty?"

She nodded. "Yes. You are feeling guilty you weren't as badly injured as the others. Guilty that Cole was suffering more than you. That Brock suffered and that so many others here are suffering. Look at you. Can you focus on your own healing as much as you focused on helping everyone else? It's not that you're purposely running yourself ragged, but how many times, at the end of the day, do I come see you, and you're exhausted? Sure, I know Shane's workouts take a toll on you. All of your rehab does. But I'm sure you are also popping into almost every room to give words of encouragement to others."

His eyebrows rose. "And that can't be just my natural personality?"

This time a note of defensiveness was in his tone. One she recognized. "Of course it can," she said gently. "But it's also important to make sure you're not doing it to absolve yourself of any guilt because these men are suffering more than you ever did."

His pinched face meant she had crossed the line. She still hadn't learned to keep her mouth shut. She said, "I didn't mean to take the conversation in that direction. You can take the parts that fit and disregard the rest."

She gave him a quick smile. "And now I'm getting chilled, so I'll take these dishes to Dennis and go to my room for the night." She stood, collected all the dishes, and headed to the stairs with her tray. When she was halfway up, she glanced back. He hadn't moved.

He sat there, staring at the table.

"Have a good night," she called out.

Back in the dining hall, she placed the tray onto the rack of dirty dishes and then headed to her studio apartment.

If she felt bad before, she felt terrible now. She had a quick hot shower, dried off, and changed into her pajamas. Then she crawled into bed and turned off the light.

"You're a fool, Hannah. A complete fool," she whispered to the darkness.

She rolled over and tried to fall asleep. But before long, she knew there would be no sleep for her. She was filled with guilt. What she'd said ate at her. Finally, she grabbed her phone, pulled up his Contact and wrote a quick text.

I'm so sorry.

And she sent it. Instantly, she felt better. She wasn't a mean person. She hated to hurt anybody, yet there was no way to ignore the fact she had hurt him.

There was no immediate response, and she realized he'd probably gone to bed. That was exactly what she should do too. She pulled up her blankets and closed her eyes and fell into an uneasy sleep. When her phone jingled, she came out of her doze and fumbled for the device.

It was Denton.

"Don't be sorry. You spoke the truth. It wasn't easy to swallow some of it. That doesn't mean it was the wrong thing to do. I only hope the reason you saw that in me wasn't because you see something similar in yourself. Because that would mean you had suffered and that's not something I would want for you."

She burst into tears. Even now he was only thinking of her.

"No, I didn't, other than losing my best friend," she quickly replied through her tears, "and what I've seen in my years of observing. Maybe I better learn to keep my mouth shut."

He replied, "Not an issue. So don't make it one and definitely don't consider quitting."

She sniffled. "It might be better if I do."

"If it's the job, that's one thing," he said. "But please stay in touch. I don't want to lose you too."

She cocked her head at the odd phrase. "What do you mean by *me too*?"

"Being in the military," he said, "we lost a lot of people I worked with. Some died. Others were too badly injured to continue, and some couldn't handle the pressure, and they just left. That's one of the reasons why I work hard to be a good friend—because I've lost so many. I don't want to lose any more."

"Are we friends? Is that what this is?" she asked. "It seems like it's so much more." She took a deep breath, then let the words out. "And yet, at the same time so much less."

"I'M SORRY," HE said in a low voice. "I'll take the blame for that."

There was silence, and he winced. This wasn't quite how he'd wanted the conversation to go. He wanted things between them to be light and heartwarming. And then he realized what he had told her, about him being friends with her. Should he correct that now? Maybe it would be easier over the phone to not see any rejection on her face.

"I want this to be so much more," he said. "It has the makings to be more. It can be warm and caring and loving. But I understand that you already have somebody else in your life who you are attracted to. And that's not something I want to interfere with."

Her broken laugh made his wince deepen.

"Sure, and that person is you. But I felt like I was nothing more than a friend, and isn't that ironic? Because what I wanted was to be more than friends. Seeing you and your friends, I wanted to be a part of that. And in a way, you have become my friend. Once I realized that, I wanted so much more."

He grinned. "Then why are we having this conversation over the phone?" he said in a bright tone. "We could be sitting together, having coffee, or curled up in bed, discussing our feelings."

"I'm not very good at discussing my feelings," she said with a note of defiance.

"Neither am I." He gave a laugh. "You do realize how ridiculous this conversation is? Like we're dragging this information out of each other."

"You should be getting some sleep. You need to heal tonight so you have a good day tomorrow."

"What? Are you hanging up on me? This is a perfect opportunity to have a little bit of intimacy."

"It is?"

He could hear the cautious question in her voice. "It is," he said affirmatively. "Only somebody who's been posted on missions all over the world understands how important it is to keep a relationship going over long distances. Only somebody like that can understand how important it is to use whatever medium is available to stay in touch, to keep that connection alive, even though they're miles away."

"Oh."

He shook his head, smiling to himself. "You really are sweet."

That startled a laugh out of her. "That's the last thing I am. Pragmatic, yes. Realistic, yes, and reserved, yes."

"Sweet, yes. Innocent in so many ways, yes. Caring, yes. Even now you're telling me to go to sleep so I have a better day tomorrow."

"It's important. That's what you're here for."

"I'm here for a lot of reasons. Physical healing is one of them. But that doesn't mean I should turn my back on something else that's so very important."

"What is that?"

"You." He heard her gasp, and then her voice became soft and tender.

"You mean that?"

"Absolutely."

141

"Oh. Well, in that case, you still need to get some sleep, and I think we should meet for breakfast. See if you wake up with a completely different mind-set. I'm sure the light of reality and the bright day will change your mind."

He shook his head and gave a bark of laughter. "Skittish, I like that." He had no idea why because, in many ways, it was foolish. But something about her always pulling back from a relationship with him was refreshing. It wasn't that he wanted to give chase, but she wasn't just diving in, happy to have known him for five minutes.

He'd seen a ton of relationships like that. Short-term. He'd always planned on growing old with somebody, planned on staying with the right person for the rest of his life. He couldn't imagine anything nicer than taking the next sixty years and exploring the world around them but also the world between them. There was so much to learn when you were with somebody new. Their perspective was different. Their feelings were different. Just the way they comprehended life around them was different. So many people tried to make those perceptions bend and twist to fit their own ways, but he was the opposite.

He wanted to see what the other person had to offer and to learn from it. There was such joy, such freedom, in that. With a smile on his face, he said his goodbyes, hung up the phone and snuggled under the covers. He was reminded once more that coming here had been the best decision he'd ever made. And for once, that decision had nothing to do with Brock and Cole.

Chapter 14

HANNAH WOKE WITH a smile on her face and a bounce to her step. Inside, however, she had a case of nerves. And then she realized she'd overslept. She raced through her shower and got dressed, and by then, it was time to meet Denton for breakfast, and she felt rushed and panicked. Not the cool, calm, capable woman she preferred to present. Instead, she bolted for the dining room in a mad rush. The last thing she wanted him to think was that she had stood him up.

Of course, he was already there, sitting at a table for two out in the sunshine. He had a cup of coffee in his hand and a smile on his face. She grinned and made her way to him. She sat down. "Sorry I'm late."

He raised his eyebrows. "You're not late. I'm early."

She glanced at her watch and realized she was five minutes early too. She settled back in her chair. "Well."

He chuckled. "I'll take that as a good sign on both our parts."

She leaned over and held out her hand. He picked hers up in his and entwined their fingers. She stared down at them. "Are we thinking that something might be here?"

"I never had a problem with the whole friendship thing. I needed to understand my motivations behind my actions," he admitted. "And now I have to take another look at my motivations for maybe not working quite so hard. So I can stay here longer to spend more time with you."

He had said the words in a joking manner, but she realized he was at least partially serious. She laughed. "I don't want you doing that. But after you've healed and no longer live here, if you were to find a job or a vocation not too far away, then I won't object to that."

He nodded. "I'm giving serious thought to that."

"Any ideas?"

He shook his head. "No, not yet. But I have some friends I can talk to. One is a developer in town. He tried to recruit me before."

"In Dallas?"

He nodded. "Yes. He does those large multi-building, multi-floor apartments and business high-rises."

"What would you do?"

He shrugged. "One of the things I was well-known for in the military, and even before, was getting the job done. So I think he sees me as not quite a project manager but maybe the manager over project managers."

She whistled. "Wow, starting right at the top."

He shook his head and grinned. "What I get to do is kick butt. Only not military style anymore."

"I'm beginning to see how different that is," she said seriously. "The navy and all the other military branches have a pretty tough regimen when it comes to forcing people to do what needs to be done. The fact that you were a US Navy SEAL, well, that adds to my admiration for what you went through."

He shook his head. "But now I have to deal with something different. And that's a whole other story."

She chuckled. "Nope, you are one of those bright friendly guys in every light."

"Until I'm the one who takes your job away because you can't do the job yourself."

She winced. "Okay, I haven't seen that side of you, but I don't doubt it's there. I couldn't do it. I'd have trouble firing anybody. But I make a great team player."

"That's one thing I do understand—teamwork. So it's an interesting prospect."

"It would keep you close?"

He nodded. "Thomas has ten years of work ahead of him at least. He's really buried. He could use an extra hand."

"But can't he hand over control to somebody else?"

He shot her a look of respect. "That's the problem I was thinking about. Thomas has the tendency to be scatter-brained, and he needs somebody to keep him organized too. Anyway, he might come by to talk to me in a week or two. I need more details about the job itself, the hours, and of course, the paycheck."

"For something like that, it would probably be at least twice what you were paid in the military."

His eyebrows shot up. "I know the private sector pays a lot more money, but I doubt it would be anything like that."

"Developers will pay big bucks from what I hear. Particularly if you're any good, then you can write your own ticket. Because having capable managers who can get the job done will save them time—stop them from having to step in and deal with the crap—and save them money for delays and overruns." She studied him carefully. "You know? I think you'd do well at that. You're personable, but you have an iron will." She gave him a nod. "You'd excel at that."

"I don't have any training though. I may have to take some courses or something." He shrugged and stared down at his coffee cup. "Not sure yet."

"And no need to rush forward into a decision. You're here for at least another two months, and then decision time will happen. But not today, not right now."

"Exactly." He lifted his coffee cup in a toast. "Well, should we get some food?"

She glanced over at the buffet, showing some signs of activity. "Sure. You know? I think we both should go." She glanced back at him. "Are you coming?"

"Absolutely."

Together they walked over and selected their breakfast foods. Hannah grabbed a coffee while she was there and then deliberately turned her back on Denton, letting him know she could give him the space he needed to be independent, and returned to their table. And as she had expected, he had followed behind her with his own tray, encountering no problems.

"You're getting very adept at handling independence."

He nodded. "I'm more confident about that now. I may have always been fairly good at it."

"Plus making friends," she teased.

"Friends have always been a major part of my support group." He took several bites of scrambled egg, then lifted his head. "By the way, I'd like to be included in those day trips into town."

"We're doing two a month. I'll put you down for the next one if you like. They've become hugely popular. People making friends all over the place," she added with a smile.

He chuckled. "Fun trips will do that."

They settled into an easy camaraderie and finished breakfast. Both Cole and Brock walked over and sat down with them, their elbows on the table, glancing from Hannah to Denton. She could feel the heat climbing her neck. She pushed her chair back. "I'll go grab more coffee." She looked at Denton. "Shall I refill yours?"

He handed her his cup, and she walked away. She didn't know why she was uncomfortable with Brock and Cole, except for her earlier motivations and thinking maybe getting close to the women would allow her into that group too—and of course, they likely blamed her for Denton cooling his relationship with Brock and Cole.

So very twisted of her. And her mind acknowledged—so very human. As she looked over her shoulder, the men still sat there. She wasn't sure what to think about that, but she knew she needed to get used to it. These three were all very close. And of course, it was natural for them to want to check her out and make sure she was good enough for Denton. Something that she probably failed at right from the beginning.

With both cups refilled, she returned to the table, surprised and a little unsettled to join all three of them there.

She gave Brock and Cole as friendly a smile as she could muster. "How are you two doing?"

Cole answered. "Good. We're checking to make sure our buddy here is doing as well as he can."

She nodded and kept her voice neutral. "As you can see, he's doing well," she said warmly, her gaze darting to Denton and back again.

He reached across the table and covered her hand with one of his.

The men's gazes went from one to the other, and then Brock spoke up. "We're glad to see this."

She glanced at him in surprise. "Why? I thought you were upset over the relationship."

Brock shook his head. "Only when we thought you were trying to separate him from us." He gave her a boyish grin. "But we understand now, and so we think you two will do well together."

Totally surprised at his unexpected response, she stared at him. "Why would you think that?" she asked cautiously.

He grinned. "Because he's very friendly, and you're very reserved, so you'll help tone down the puppy in him, and he'll help bring out the puppy in you."

Her jaw dropped. And then she chuckled. "I'm not sure if that sounds like an adult relationship or not, but it does sound like fun."

"And more fun is definitely required. Something about this place encourages effort, serious determination and focus, but we all need to let our hair down sometimes, and we all need someone to do that with."

How true. And yet, she wanted so much more. As she glanced over at Denton, she squeezed his hand and watched his gaze light up.

She wondered if she'd ever get tired of seeing that look in his eyes. That sense that they were on the same page, connected in ways she didn't understand. Lord, she hoped she wouldn't.

Then he dropped her hand. "There is nothing quite so special as friends."

And *wham*, she'd been friend-zoned—again.

DENTON CAUGHT AN odd look on Brock's face and realized he had said the wrong thing. Had she noticed? Did she understand?

Brock and Cole were his friends, but that didn't mean Denton wanted his buddies to know how close he was getting to Hannah. For that reason he had pulled back, dropping her hand.

Hannah stood then, collected her coffee cup and said, "Back to work for me." She smiled in farewell and walked away, placing her dirty cup on the dish rack.

Denton glanced at Brock. "What was that earlier look on your face for?"

Brock settled back. "I thought I understood the relationship was much more serious than I first considered. But then you made it sound like you two were just friends, so that confused me. But maybe it's not me who is confused. It's you."

Cole spoke up. "Exactly what I would say. It's like you're hot, then cold."

Denton leaned back. "I didn't back off that badly."

Both men snorted.

"Yes, you did," Brock said. "You dropped the relationship to being just friends."

Denton glanced at his hands, realizing if that was how his actions looked to the men, it was also how it would look to her. The opposite of what he had wanted. He understood why he'd done it, but he didn't want to explain it to his buddies.

"I guess I'm a little confused." He tried to joke it off lightly.

"Understandable. Nothing like a young love to remind us that there's so much else in life, and maybe she isn't the right person for you after all." Cole shrugged. "No way to tell but to go forward and see what comes from it."

Denton thought about all the things he knew about

her—the way she acted, her honesty and caring, her integrity and he was pretty darn sure of the return of emotion. He nodded. "I'm sure she's right for me."

"You've only known her for like three weeks at most." Brock shook his head. "Don't push it."

Denton laughed. "Is that you saying that? I know you're another few months down the relationship road with the love of your life, but it didn't take you long to figure out what you wanted. I'd hate to think I'm that slow." The thing is, he wasn't. He knew what he wanted—Hannah.

But it was new and not something he wanted to share or have his friends criticize.

"It's not that you're slow, but I think it has to do with all this friends stuff that she's got you thinking about. That appears to confuse the issue for you."

Good point. He frowned. "How do I know if her friendship is more than friendship?"

"You already know you're more than friends. The question is, how much more? The thing is, you don't have to answer that now. You take a few steps down that road and see how it feels, see what develops, see how it grows."

"We've been dancing around the issue of coming together, separating, coming together ... It's been a unique time."

"Partly because you're injured, partly because she works here. So you have a lot of different issues that will be affected. Have you discussed the future at all?" Brock pressed.

Denton nodded. "We were talking about me hooking up with Thomas's company in Dallas." They already knew about his friend, had met him over the years.

"Did that make her happy?" Cole asked.

Denton smiled and nodded. "Yes."

150

"Good," Brock said. "Then don't analyze it too much. Just let it happen. You'll do fine." He stood up and grinned at Denton. "I'm really happy for you."

The men left soon afterward. Inasmuch as Denton appreciated their parting words of wisdom, he couldn't stop the feeling that he'd done something very wrong. Or that Hannah would take his actions the wrong way.

He stared at his phone. Nope. It would be better to explain in person. He should go to her office, which was something he rarely did. He thought about that for a long moment and realized he avoided her work environment. He didn't want to intrude with her work the same way she didn't intrude on his life here because he was one of the patients.

Decision made, he got up and walked to her office. "You left rather abruptly," he said quietly. "I came to see if something was wrong."

If he hadn't been watching her face so closely, he wouldn't have seen the hurt whisper across her features.

"I didn't mean to hurt you or make it seem to you like we were only friends, *only* to my buddies," he quickly added. "I didn't think about how you'd perceive it until you got up and left." Wisely, he withheld mentioning Brock and Cole's responses.

She shot him a shuttered look.

He sighed. "I don't want a relationship where I constantly have to worry about what I say, afraid you will take it the wrong way. I would never do anything to hurt you, and I would never do anything deliberately to make you feel bad. If you feel like I relegated our relationship back to friends, I'm sorry because that hadn't been my intention."

She studied him for a long moment. "Yet, that's what it

seemed like. And here I'd thought we'd moved past that."

He nodded. "We have. And it feels ... I don't know ... special."

At her start of surprise, he tried to explain. "I wanted to keep it between us. Enjoy knowing we're together. They are my friends, but I don't tell them every single thing. I was afraid that if I told them about us, about how I felt, in some way it would take away the intimacy, the uniqueness of what we have."

Her gaze warmed. She sat back in her chair and stared at him in surprise. "So, you were trying to distance them, not me?"

He thought about that for a long moment, then nodded. "That's probably a good way to look at it." He shrugged and gave her a sheepish look. "They know so much about me that they already understand how close we are. But I didn't want to discuss it with them. I wanted to keep it just for us, something between us for as long as I could."

Slowly a smile dawned across her face, and he relaxed, but his gaze was caught on how special her smile was. And he was so damn glad it was just for him.

"It's probably the one excuse any woman would accept—and be delighted with." She chuckled. "And in this case, you're completely forgiven."

He laughed and mimicked wiping sweat off his face. "I fully expect I will make more mistakes, you know?" he warned. "Please don't hold them against me and walk away hurt. I will do my best not to blunder, and I will do everything in my power to not make the same mistakes again."

Chapter 15

HANNAH SMILED UP at him. She had been hurt, but his explanation more than made up for it. "Apparently," she said, "I have more to learn in this relationship than you do."

He grinned at her. "Then how about we teach each other?"

Denton opened his arms, and Hannah stood and stepped into them. For the first time, she didn't care if anybody could see. She didn't worry what others might think or about getting into trouble. Or raised eyebrows at her unorthodox behavior. This was good. And she'd do a lot to fight for it.

Actually, she'd do anything. He was the one man for her. The road wouldn't be calm or straightforward, but she'd never been one to take the easy road in anything she did.

Over Denton's shoulder, she caught Dani glancing up to see the two of them hugging. A big smile flashed across her face, and she gave Hannah the thumbs-up sign.

Hannah pulled back slightly. "Don't look now, but our relationship is no longer a secret."

Denton twisted slightly. Several people were peering through the open doorway, wide grins on their faces, followed by Dani, who got up and walked from her office with a wave and a smile.

Hannah chuckled. "My vote is to give them something really juicy to look at. Then no one will have any doubts we're together."

"I'm all for that." He tilted up her chin and pulled her into his arms for a passionate kiss.

She threw her arms around his neck and kissed him back.

A kiss full of promise. A kiss full of love. A kiss not just for the moment but forever.

Epilogue

E LLIOT CARVER STARED at the letter on his lap. He'd
avoided opening it for the last thirty minutes. It was
from Hathaway House and—with any luck—Aaron Ham-
mond himself.

He still wasn't sure he should go, even if a room was
available. He'd come to realize that nothing anyone could do
would likely help him out. A change of scenery would be
good, and if he could make a change, then this would be the
best option.

If it was an option.

He'd known Aaron in the military, and like Elliot, Aaron had been injured. Hathaway House had turned his life
around to the point that he was now engaged to Dani
Hathaway, part owner and manager of the rehabilitation
center.

Aaron had been instrumental in bringing in other people, others of the US Navy SEAL brotherhood who were in
need. Then the men who served helped each other rehab.
And if you were a SEAL, then the hand was held out even
farther.

But what if Elliot wasn't qualified or didn't fit or failed
to meet their medical requirements? So many aspects could
mess this up for him. Including his own doubts ...

"Aren't you going to open your mail?" Finn asked, rolling to his side. He was a maverick, like Elliot. Only Elliot felt washed up and thrown away. Finn was new to rehab. New to being injured. He was in a holding pattern, but he had a mess of surgeries coming up. If he kept his positive outlook on life after all that, then Elliot would be happier for Finn. As it were, if Elliot himself could get some sleep, then maybe life would turn around for him.

Right now that looked doubtful.

He shook his head and said, "Maybe later."

"Hell, no way. You open that. If this works out for you, then maybe I'll give the place a try. We have to stick together. This is a battle we didn't train for, so it'll take all the intel we can get to make it through."

A groan escaped. Finn was right. Elliot suddenly reached down and snatched up the envelope. If he got an invitation to go, yeah, he would go. All the rest was his fear talking.

And he'd had enough of that crap. *All in, all the time.* The SEAL motto he now used like a mantra.

He ripped it open and pulled out the letter.

His heart slammed against his ribs as he read the first line out loud.

"Elliot, we'd like to invite you to Hathaway House for the rest of your rehabilitation ..."

"Hot damn," Finn crowed with envy. "Go and then tell me how it is. I'll get started on my own request."

Elliot stared at his friend and knew Finn was right about one thing. This journey was one none of them had experienced before. They had to learn from those who had gone before.

"Do it," Elliot said, waving the acceptance letter in his hand. "I'll meet you there, and we'll both beat this."

And the two men shook hands about their future.

This concludes Book 4 of Hathaway House: Denton.
Read about Elliot: Hathaway House, Book 5

Hathaway House: Elliot (Book #5)

Welcome to Hathaway House. Rehab Center. Safe Haven. Second chance at life and love.

Former Navy SEAL Elliot Carver came to Hathaway House to get help with the lingering repercussions of a mission gone bad. His body is dealing with the physical trauma of a spinal cord injury, while his mind is caught in a loop of painful memories that he can't sideline, and both won't let him heal the way he'd like.

Former ER Nurse Sicily Lawrence has just made her way out of a difficult relationship, and the quietness of the night shift at Hathaway House gives her peace of mind. The last thing she needs is to get involved in another volatile union. But she has seen injuries like Elliot's before, and she knows that a certain type of therapy can help. One Elliot isn't interested in trying.

Now, for Elliot's sake, Sicily must push him toward the progress he needs, even it means losing him. And, with time and luck, maybe they can cross the hurdle and find each other at Hathaway House.

Book 5 is available now!

To find out more visit Dale Mayer's website.

http://smarturl.it/ElliotDMUniversal

Author's Note

Thank you for reading Denton: Hathaway House, Book 4! If you enjoyed the book, please take a moment and leave a short review.

Dear reader,

I love to hear from readers, and you can contact me at my website: www.dalemayer.com or at my Facebook author page. To be informed of new releases and special offers, sign up for my newsletter or follow me on BookBub. And if you are interested in joining Dale Mayer's Reader Group, here is the Facebook sign up page. facebook.com/groups/402384989872660

Cheers,
Dale Mayer

Get THREE Free Books Now!

Have you met the SEALS of Honor?

SEALs of Honor Books 1, 2, and 3. Follow the stories of brave, badass warriors who serve their country with honor and love their women to the limits of life and death.

Read Mason, Hawk, and Dane right now for FREE.

Go here and tell me where to send them!
http://smarturl.it/EthanBofB

About the Author

Dale Mayer is a USA Today bestselling author best known for her Psychic Visions and Family Blood Ties series. Her contemporary romances are raw and full of passion and emotion (Second Chances, SKIN), her thrillers will keep you guessing (By Death series), and her romantic comedies will keep you giggling (It's a Dog's Life and Charmin Marvin Romantic Comedy series).

She honors the stories that come to her – and some of them are crazy and break all the rules and cross multiple genres!

To go with her fiction, she also writes nonfiction in many different fields with books available on resume writing, companion gardening and the US mortgage system. She has recently published her Career Essentials Series. All her books are available in print and ebook format.

Connect with Dale Mayer Online

Dale's Website – www.dalemayer.com

Twitter – @DaleMayer

Facebook – dalemayer.com/fb

BookBub – bookbub.com/authors/dale-mayer

Also by Dale Mayer

Published Adult Books:

Hathaway House
Aaron, Book 1
Brock, Book 2
Cole, Book 3
Denton, Book 4
Elliot, Book 5
Finn, Book 6

The K9 Files
Ethan, Book 1
Pierce, Book 2
Zane, Book 3
Blaze, Book 4
Lucas, Book 5
Parker, Book 6
Carter, Book 7

Lovely Lethal Gardens
Arsenic in the Azaleas, Book 1
Bones in the Begonias, Book 2
Corpse in the Carnations, Book 3
Daggers in the Dahlias, Book 4
Evidence in the Echinacea, Book 5
Footprints in the Ferns, Book 6

Psychic Vision Series
Tuesday's Child
Hide 'n Go Seek
Maddy's Floor
Garden of Sorrow
Knock Knock…
Rare Find
Eyes to the Soul
Now You See Her
Shattered
Into the Abyss
Seeds of Malice
Eye of the Falcon
Itsy-Bitsy Spider
Unmasked
Deep Beneath
From the Ashes
Psychic Visions Books 1–3
Psychic Visions Books 4–6
Psychic Visions Books 7–9

By Death Series
Touched by Death
Haunted by Death
Chilled by Death
By Death Books 1–3

Broken Protocols – Romantic Comedy Series
Cat's Meow
Cat's Pajamas
Cat's Cradle
Cat's Claus
Broken Protocols 1-4

Broken and... Mending
Skin
Scars
Scales (of Justice)
Broken but... Mending 1-3

Glory
Genesis
Tori
Celeste
Glory Trilogy

Biker Blues
Morgan: Biker Blues, Volume 1
Cash: Biker Blues, Volume 2

SEALs of Honor
Mason: SEALs of Honor, Book 1
Hawk: SEALs of Honor, Book 2
Dane: SEALs of Honor, Book 3
Swede: SEALs of Honor, Book 4
Shadow: SEALs of Honor, Book 5
Cooper: SEALs of Honor, Book 6
Markus: SEALs of Honor, Book 7
Evan: SEALs of Honor, Book 8
Mason's Wish: SEALs of Honor, Book 9
Chase: SEALs of Honor, Book 10
Brett: SEALs of Honor, Book 11
Devlin: SEALs of Honor, Book 12
Easton: SEALs of Honor, Book 13
Ryder: SEALs of Honor, Book 14
Macklin: SEALs of Honor, Book 15
Corey: SEALs of Honor, Book 16

Warrick: SEALs of Honor, Book 17
Tanner: SEALs of Honor, Book 18
Jackson: SEALs of Honor, Book 19
Kanen: SEALs of Honor, Book 20
Nelson: SEALs of Honor, Book 21
SEALs of Honor, Books 1–3
SEALs of Honor, Books 4–6
SEALs of Honor, Books 7–10
SEALs of Honor, Books 11–13
SEALs of Honor, Books 14–16
SEALs of Honor, Books 17–19

Heroes for Hire

Levi's Legend: Heroes for Hire, Book 1
Stone's Surrender: Heroes for Hire, Book 2
Merk's Mistake: Heroes for Hire, Book 3
Rhodes's Reward: Heroes for Hire, Book 4
Flynn's Firecracker: Heroes for Hire, Book 5
Logan's Light: Heroes for Hire, Book 6
Harrison's Heart: Heroes for Hire, Book 7
Saul's Sweetheart: Heroes for Hire, Book 8
Dakota's Delight: Heroes for Hire, Book 9
Michael's Mercy (Part of Sleeper SEAL Series)
Tyson's Treasure: Heroes for Hire, Book 10
Jace's Jewel: Heroes for Hire, Book 11
Rory's Rose: Heroes for Hire, Book 12
Brandon's Bliss: Heroes for Hire, Book 13
Liam's Lily: Heroes for Hire, Book 14
North's Nikki: Heroes for Hire, Book 15
Anders's Angel: Heroes for Hire, Book 16
Reyes's Raina: Heroes for Hire, Book 17
Dezi's Diamond: Heroes for Hire, Book 18

Vince's Vixen: Heroes for Hire, Book 19
Heroes for Hire, Books 1–3
Heroes for Hire, Books 4–6
Heroes for Hire, Books 7–9
Heroes for Hire, Books 10–12
Heroes for Hire, Books 13–15

SEALs of Steel
Badger: SEALs of Steel, Book 1
Erick: SEALs of Steel, Book 2
Cade: SEALs of Steel, Book 3
Talon: SEALs of Steel, Book 4
Laszlo: SEALs of Steel, Book 5
Geir: SEALs of Steel, Book 6
Jager: SEALs of Steel, Book 7
The Final Reveal: SEALs of Steel, Book 8
SEALs of Steel, Books 1–4
SEALs of Steel, Books 5–8
SEALs of Steel, Books 1–8

Collections
Dare to Be You...
Dare to Love...
Dare to be Strong...
RomanceX3

Standalone Novellas
It's a Dog's Life
Riana's Revenge
Second Chances

Published Young Adult Books:

Family Blood Ties Series
Vampire in Denial

Vampire in Distress

Vampire in Design

Vampire in Deceit

Vampire in Defiance

Vampire in Conflict

Vampire in Chaos

Vampire in Crisis

Vampire in Control

Vampire in Charge

Family Blood Ties Set 1–3

Family Blood Ties Set 1–5

Family Blood Ties Set 4–6

Family Blood Ties Set 7–9

Sian's Solution, A Family Blood Ties Series Prequel
    Novelette

Design series
Dangerous Designs

Deadly Designs

Darkest Designs

Design Series Trilogy

Standalone
In Cassie's Corner

Gem Stone (a Gemma Stone Mystery)

Time Thieves

Published Non-Fiction Books:

Career Essentials

Career Essentials: The Résumé
Career Essentials: The Cover Letter
Career Essentials: The Interview
Career Essentials: 3 in 1